MAYDAY

MAYDAY

KAREN HARRINGTON

SCHOLASTIC INC.

ISBN 978-1-338-11700-4

Copyright © 2016 by Karen Harrington. All rights reserved.
Published by Scholastic Inc., 557 Broadway, New York, NY 10012, by arrangement with Little, Brown Books for Young Readers, a division of Hachette Book Group, Inc. SCHOLASTIC and associated logos are trademarks and/or registered trademarks of Scholastic Inc.

12 11 10 9 8 7 6 5 4 3 2 1   16 17 18 19 20 21

Printed in the U.S.A.   40

First Scholastic printing, November 2016

For my grandfather and father,
who served our country, and all those brave
members of the U.S. military, past and present.
Thank you.

CHAPTER 1

Listen, I didn't want to talk about poinsettias in the first place. But if I recite a fact, it is the fact talking, not me. A fact is like a shield. You can hide behind it. Then you can make a run for it if you need to. Or make someone laugh so that they aren't laughing at you. Or distract your mom if she is sad.

From fourth grade on, I made myself absorb facts the way a sponge absorbs water.

So when I tell you that I really didn't *want* to talk about poinsettias in front of my uncle right before he deployed for the third time last September, I'm telling you the truth. But a fact had to fill the uncomfortable space. He was staring into his cheeseburger like it was a movie screen. I didn't know what to do.

So I said to my uncle, "Did you know the red poinsettia originated in Mexico and is named after Joel Roberts Poinsett, the first United States minister to Mexico? That's lucky, because what if his last name was Frankenbucket? Then at Christmas everyone would have to say, *Here, I brought you this Frankenbuckettia*."

He smiled. Uncle Reed was my mom's brother and an army soldier. When he came home, I never really knew what to say to him.

"No, I didn't know that about poinsettias, Wayne," Uncle Reed said. "I bet your brain can fire at will with random facts."

I couldn't be sure, but I thought he meant that as a compliment.

I hoped he meant it as a compliment.

"I meant that as a compliment," he finally said. "So, did you want to talk about poinsettias?"

No, I didn't *want* to talk about poinsettias.

But I'd had to find a new topic. Another truth? Inserting a quick fact will change the subject. You can go from uncomfortable to learning something new in 5.6 seconds.

Uncle Reed had been talking about Iraq. He said it was hard to come back home to Texas. "I need to be with my buddies. When I'm home, I feel like I should be there. Helping."

I couldn't work out why he didn't prefer being at home.

Uncle Reed got a far-off look in his eyes. "I get a different feeling about myself when I'm there. A useful feeling. A real sense of purpose." That part of what Uncle Reed said made sense. Being useful is important in our family.

I swirled a french fry in my ketchup. "I don't even understand why soldiers still have to keep going back to Iraq," I said. "Why is it taking so long?"

"Your problem, Wayne, is that you always ask why. Some questions can't be answered."

"Why?"

He looked down. "The question *why* will plague you for your entire life."

I definitely didn't want to be plagued for my entire life. The past month was plaguing enough. Why did Sandy Showalter *really* go with me to the fall social? Why was my mom suddenly encouraging me to spend more time with my dad?

"I have more questions than answers," I said. "I hate that."

"Join the club," he said, laughing. "One more piece of advice: Never eat at any place ending in the words *corral* or *barn*. The food at those establishments is all beige."

He took a drink from his iced tea. The silence hung over us like a rotten smell. So I'd searched my brain for a new topic. Why poinsettias? Because Beatty Middle School's orchestra was in the middle of a fund-raiser. *(Pre-order your holiday poinsettia now and help the Beatty Bears get to Colorado for spring break!)* Sandy Showalter was in the Beatty Bears orchestra. I ordered four poinsettias.

Uncle Reed drummed his fingers on the table. He didn't look so happy. He didn't want to talk about poinsettias. His mind was someplace else. Maybe with his friends in Iraq. I tried a new topic.

"So your friend Schmidt is pretty brave, then? Four deployments in, right?"

He slapped his hand on the tabletop. "Brave as the first man who ate an oyster."

"Grandpa always says that," I said. "It's lame."

"Well, where do you think I heard it first? Plus, I mean, a slimy oyster. Think about it. That's some brave eating." He was smiling now.

"I bet some eighth grader probably dared him to do it," I said. That made Uncle Reed laugh like crazy.

"Middle school doesn't last forever, Wayne," he said. "You'll make it. You'll be a good soldier one day." He looked at me straight on then. I had to look away.

I couldn't see myself as a soldier. You had to be brave, have courage in your blood. Grandpa said that, too. *All Daltons have courage in their blood!*

4

Well, my name is Wayne Kovok. I am half Dalton, half Kovok. Maybe I had only half the courage. The way Grandpa looked at me sometimes made me wonder if he was thinking the same thing. Probably.

"Are you going to eat all your fries?" Uncle Reed asked. "Because I do miss fries. A lot."

"Take them." I pushed my basket of fries across the table.

"Thank you," he said. "In exchange for these delicious fries, I will give you a story. A true story, because I know my nephew likes those best."

It was true. I liked a good true story.

This is what he told me.

In 2010, a guy boarded a twenty-seat prop plane in the Congo with a crocodile hidden in a duffel bag.

The crocodile escaped. The passengers panicked. Nineteen of them rushed toward the cockpit, sending the plane off balance. The sudden weight imbalance caused the pilot to lose control. The plane cartwheeled in the air and then crashed into an empty house.

Nineteen passengers and the pilot died.

There were two survivors. One passenger and the crocodile.

"Wait, what? The crocodile survived?" I asked. This didn't seem like a true story.

"I'm not lying. It really happened. The crocodile survived. Probably because it didn't panic."

"A crocodile doesn't know enough to be panicked." I'd spoken as if this were a fact. I would look it up later to verify. My knowledge of panic and animals was limited.

"Exactly," Reed said. "Panic leads to disaster."

"You do realize you're getting on a plane tomorrow, right?" Sure, I liked a weird story, but even I wouldn't talk about a plane crash before boarding an actual plane. My fact-spewing weirdness has a few boundaries.

"I know, but it reminds me that I have no control over life. Life doesn't care if you're a soldier or a seventh grader or an aquatic reptile. Things happen. Are you going to finish your burger?"

Uncle Reed finished my burger. I think he must have missed burgers when he was far from home, too.

"I sure miss burgers when I'm away from home," he said.

I sat there thinking about the crocodile, the plane cartwheeling in the air, the crash. The whole story was so strange. What would it feel like to be in a plane, falling toward the ground? Would stuff be tossed around inside the fuselage? Would people scream? What did passengers think about right before impact?

I had so many questions. I mean, who wouldn't? Who

wouldn't be curious about what it's like inside a doomed plane?

Now you can get the answers by looking them up. That's the easy way. I personally recommend that method. I do not recommend gathering the data by being an actual plane-crash survivor.

That's the hard way. That's the way I did it. I became like the plane-crash-surviving crocodile.

How?

Well, after Uncle Reed went on his next deployment, I went on the biggest trip of my life. I went to sleep in my native land of BEFORE, where I'd lived all twelve and a half years of my life. And then I woke up with no left eyebrow, with stitches down my face, wearing only socks and a backless gown in a country called AFTER. And in this new country, I couldn't talk.

True story.

Do you know how awkward it is to be a plane-crash-surviving, fact-collecting seventh grader with no voice to use as a shield?

Pretty awkward.

BEFORE

CHAPTER 2

A lot had to happen before I went on the biggest trip of my life. A lot had to happen before that guy in the Congo had the not-so-bright idea to put a crocodile in his duffel bag and board the plane, right?

Because the number one fact of being a plane-crash survivor is this: You must be on a plane. You needed a reason to fly.

A seventh grader like me didn't have a whole lot of reasons to fly. My family lives in Texas. All of them. My mom is single and we aren't exactly rich. Our idea of taking a vacation was driving down to Galveston or hanging out at Six Flags for the day. That was it.

It was an October Friday in the land of BEFORE. One of those really great days where the air was beginning to cool and you just wanted to take big gulps of it. It would be the day I got my reason to fly.

I was late to the bus. I was late to the bus every day ending in the letter *y*. I'd eat my cereal at the kitchen table and try to load up on a few new facts so that I'd have something to say to Sandy Showalter. I couldn't risk having nothing to say to her. Better a fact than an awkward silence.

Everyone was pretty crazy on the bus that morning. I got Carl, the bus driver, to yell at me for being late.

"You gonna do this every day, Kovok?" he asked. His eyebrows rose.

"Carl, did you know everyone has a unique tongue print, just like fingerprints?" Carl was usually the beneficiary of my first fact of the day. I liked to try them out on him first.

"It's against company policy to call you weird, Kovok," he said. "Take your seat."

I wouldn't have minded if he called me weird. I considered it a compliment.

So I got to my seat, dodging a few flying erasers and one mystery object. I hoped I hadn't perspired too much during the run. I had precalculated the amount of Axe body spray I needed to use to make me smell acceptable by the time Sandy arrived. Two and a half sprays. That's the right amount. Anything more over-powers the bus. You learn this in sixth grade when a mean eighth-grade girl says, "You smell like you want to be alone."

True story.

By the time Sandy, the prettiest girl in seventh grade, boarded the bus, I was breathing steady. Smoothing my hair back. Putting on a brave face.

Did you know the prettiest girl in seventh grade went to the fall social with me, Wayne Kovok, three weeks earlier? Did you know that when I asked her if we were going together, she replied, "Sort of, I guess"?

Sort of.

That was a fact that had the power to distract even me! A fact I enjoyed repeating to myself often.

Sandy. Wayne. Sandy. Wayne. Sandy. Wayne. Sort of together for three weeks and four days.

Not that I was counting the days.

Sandy was a beautiful, blue-eyed, golden-haired true lover of poetry, if you want to know. Sandy was also a hero in my book. My first memory of her was when she handed me a stack of napkins in fifth grade after some jerk squirted ketchup all over my face.

You didn't forget a girl who helped you like that. A girl like that could plague you. In a good way.

That morning, she sat in the row of seats right in front of me.

"Sandy. Hey, Sandy. Sandy," I said.

"What?" Sandy said.

"Hi."

"Hi, Wayne."

"Hey."

"Did you race to the bus again?" Sandy asked.

"Yes."

"He's going to get mad."

"Whaddya gonna do?" I said.

"Why do you have to run, Wayne?" she asked.

Why do I have to run?

Why? The plaguing question.

I told myself to be quiet. Not to expand on all the running facts I knew. Or thoughts about shoelaces. Sneakers. Foot powder. Or how fast cheetahs can run.

Don't say a chicken fact! Don't say a chicken fact! "Did you know that chickens can run up to nine miles an hour?" I tried to make it sound funny. The look on Sandy's face told me I'd failed in my attempt.

"But don't humans run that fast?" Sandy asked.

"The average human jogs at an average speed of seven miles per hour," I replied, which was true.

"Oh, cool," Sandy said.

She turned around and faced the front. I saw her reflection in the window. She smiled. I tried to remember to breathe.

A chicken fact? Really?

Why didn't I just give her a simple answer?

Well, the real answer to why I ran to the bus had nothing to do with outrunning chickens. The real reason was a secret known only to me, my sneakers, and the pavement we flew over.

My dad had been a medal-winning, trophy-receiving, scholarship-earning high school track star. He dreamed of his son being a medal-winning, trophy-receiving, scholarship-earning high school track star, too. And I wanted to be like him. I really did.

So I ran because he wanted me to.

You think you'll be a track star like me, boy?

Yeah, I hoped I'd be like him.

And then in a snap, I hated running. It was because of that time he did what he did. I was eight. He made me chase his car. You know how embarrassing that is? You couldn't change some facts, even if you wanted to. Those were the facts you tried to forget.

Oh, come on, Wayne, I was just messing with you, he'd said. *Let's go get ice cream.*

Do you know how miserable it is to eat ice cream

when you feel stupid? Pretty miserable. Miserable enough to stay away from ice cream for a long time.

After that, I wanted to run *away* from him. Sometimes I looked in the mirror and saw a younger version of him: tall, skinny, dark-haired, and blue-eyed.

You couldn't run away from yourself.

So then I ran for myself sometimes. Mostly just to the bus. When I ran, I was free. And if he dared me to run again, I'd be ready.

Was this the kind of information you shared with the prettiest girl in seventh grade, who considered you her sort-of boyfriend? No way.

It was safer to go with a chicken fact.

CHAPTER 3

We filed off the bus into the Beatty Middle School parking lot. I had Spanish on my mind then, not a plane ticket. I ran Spanish phrases across my brain in preparation for my last-period Spanish quiz.

Dar un paseo	To take a walk
Ganar la carrera	To win the race

Part of the quiz involved reading and translating sentences out loud. Sandy was also in my Spanish class. I risked being a dork in another language.

"Do you want to study at lunch?" Sandy asked me as we headed through the school doors.

"*Sí*," I said. "*Eres muy bonita.*" I'd thought maybe if I

complimented Sandy in another language, it wouldn't be weird.

"What?" she asked, smiling at me.

"Nothing." It was weird. My neck turned hot and red. Even though it was an actual fact that Sandy was very pretty. Maybe I've mentioned this a time or ten.

"Later, Wayne," she said.

At lunch, I scanned the cafeteria for Sandy. She was nowhere to be seen. I figured she'd ditched me. But then I found her at *my* lunch table, where I sit with the studiers and two girls I know, Mysti and Rama. I shot them a look.

Say nothing.

They knew all about Sandy. They had coached me on what to say to her. But I needed their silence now. I put my lunch and books down. They giggled.

"Why did I even sign up for Spanish?" Sandy asked.

"Did you know that Spanish is second only to English as the most spoken language in the world? So you'll know two of the most popular languages."

Sandy smiled. *"Bueno."*

"See, you're a pro already."

"Okay, first question," Sandy said. She pulled out a neat stack of note cards. *"Me permite ir al baño, por favor?"*

" 'May I go to the bathroom, please?' "

"Good."

"Okay, your turn. *Puedo tener otro taco?*"

" 'May I have another taco?' "

"*Sí*," I said. "Do you think Señora Wilson meant that phrase to come before or after the bathroom question?"

"Very funny, Wayne," Sandy said.

It was great. We laughed and practiced until the bell rang. It was getting easier to be around Sandy. Was it possible that I could feel chilled out around her more often? That I wouldn't have to sweat facts every time I saw her? I liked that idea a lot. By the time Spanish class rolled around, I saw myself traveling to Mexico, ordering tacos and asking permission to go to the bathroom.

Señora Wilson called out each student's name as she put a piece of paper on the overhead projector. She unveiled three phrases at a time. *Uno, dos, tres.*

"Señor Kovok." The teacher called my name.

I stood up and translated my three phrases.

And then it was Sandy's turn. We smiled at each other when it was over. I drew in my notebook and let my thoughts float. I sat back in my chair and thought of the weekend.

"Señor Kovok?"

"*Sí, Señora—?*" I looked up.

The school counselor, Ms. Peet, stood in the doorway of my Spanish class. She was flanked by Mom and Grandpa.

You know how your stomach senses bad news before your ears hear it?

"Señora Wilson," the counselor said. "May we please see Mr. Kovok out in the hallway?"

My stomach rumbled.

I turned to look back at the class. Maybe everyone was staring at me. I only looked at Sandy. I caught her smile before I slipped out into the hallway.

"Wayne," Mom said. I could tell she was biting her lip and trying not to tear up. The sad face. Grandpa hugged me to his chest. My grandfather is a retired army drill sergeant. He is not a hugger.

Something was seriously wrong.

Grandpa pushed me away from his chest. He stared me down like I'd done something wrong. Like the hug had been *my* idea.

"What's wrong?" I asked. "Mom?" I thought of something I could say to change her face.

Did you know that your average tree consumes fifty to one hundred gallons of water per day?

Grandpa read my mind. "Exercise restraint, son."

I restrained.

Grandpa pushed his hands into his pockets. "Your uncle Reed has died in the line of duty."

Grandpa was steady as an oak.

Mom swayed and trembled like a new branch.

"Wait. What? What are you saying?"

"You have an agile mind, son," Grandpa said. "Don't make me repeat the words."

Sometimes bad news doesn't stick in my agile mind. I have to hear it twice. Plus, it was all wrong. Grandpa standing in my school hallway? It was out of context. Right behind him there was a giant bin of deodorants and soaps for the school hygiene drive, along with a poster that read AFRAID OF B.O.? DONATE SOME DEO!

I could have been dreaming.

"Maybe you'd like to come to my office?" Ms. Peet suggested. "Sign Wayne out for the day?"

I'd forgotten she was still standing there with us.

Grandpa said, "Wayne, why don't you be of use and gather your things on the double!"

I gathered my things on the double. It was something to do.

The bad news followed us home. I heard the sad story of how the casualty officers came to Grandpa's house.

"They read the news to me and then handed me the printed paper they'd read from," Grandpa said.

Casualty officers read the news and give you a copy of

21

the sad news, too. They do this so that their message will be clear and they won't have to repeat it.

I'd looked it up later.

Grandpa held a coffee mug in one hand and told Mom and me this story while he looked up at a picture of his own father. RB Dalton, army captain. My great-grandfather's picture hung on the hallway wall.

Did you know my mother bought this house for a wall?

Yep, she did.

When I was eight and my dad wasn't looking, Mom and I moved to this house. It was a neighborhood that wanted to be a forest. At least that was how Mom sold it to me.

"Every street here is named for a tree," she said, a little too excited.

Our house on Cedar Drive was like every other house on the block. Small, brick, and brown. Eight windows and four tiny bedrooms. Chain-link fence. And bonus feature: a hulking white water tower that loomed over our backyard.

"Well, we always said we wanted a view of the water," Mom joked. "Now we've got it! Come inside and see the best part of this house!"

The house was small. You could pretty much stand in the living room and give someone a tour just by looking left to right. Hallway with bedrooms to your left. Kitchen and dining room to your right. Garage to the back.

To her, the best part of the house was the long white wall that ran the length of the hallway.

"Would you just look at this wall?" Mom said. "It's perfect!"

I was fine with the tree-named streets and the "water" view. But when Mom fell in love with a wall, I thought she was nuts.

"I don't get it," I said.

"You will, honey."

So Mom bought the plain brown house in the shadow of a water tower in the wannabe-forest neighborhood for the perfect wall.

True story.

Before we'd unpacked a single dish on Cedar Drive, Mom hung a collage of framed photographs on that bright, perfect white wall. The Wall of Honor, she called it. It had been her dream to have all our dead military ancestors gathered in one place. My dad had nixed that idea before. He said it was stupid to hang photos of old dead people on the wall. Mom got the sad face when he said that. Around that time, Mom began referring to my dad as the Flee. (She thought I didn't know. I knew.)

It's been four years now.

But the main thing to know about the house is that Mom still *loves* that wall. I guess it's grown on me, too. I sometimes lined up my face in the eight-by-ten-inch photo with the shiny glass that featured my great-grandfather. I didn't see any connection between us, even though Mom liked to say I looked a little like him.

I knew one thing for sure: Not a single one of the photos was or ever would be a Kovok like me.

Because you had to have four qualities to be featured on that wall.

Be brave. Be patriotic. Be dead. And carry the last name Dalton. Now Uncle Reed had all four.

My whole life, I never thought the photos on the wall would mean anything to me. They could have been strangers or people in history books. Do you want to know something? It makes a difference when you can look at a picture of someone and remember you'd once shared a cheeseburger and fries. A huge difference.

When our doomed plane made its rapid descent from the sky, I thought about the last conversation I'd had with Uncle Reed. I would have done it differently. Not talked about poinsettias. But I couldn't. You don't get a do-over. And thinking about it will make you feel stupid. Helpless. You have to force yourself to do something else.

So I adjusted the frames on the wall to make them straight. Straighter.

CHAPTER 4

It was now early December in the land of BEFORE. Grandpa worked for weeks to get Uncle Reed a burial at Arlington National Cemetery. There was a waiting list for the honored dead. That might be one of the saddest facts I'd ever heard. So many soldiers needing burial that families had to wait.

While I waited I tried to be—what else?—useful. The opposite of helpless. We all did. We continued our tradition of spaghetti Tuesdays. Those were the days Grandpa came over and gave us a progress report.

"We're moving up on the list," he'd say.

And then we'd all sit around and try to act normal. I admit it was harder for Mom and Grandpa. They wore their grief like gray clothes. Everything reminded them of Reed. I had to choose my topics carefully.

"Did you know that if Cortés hadn't transported tomatoes from Mexico into Europe, we might never have had spaghetti sauce?" I asked.

"No, I didn't know that, Wayne," Mom said.

"Good spaghetti tonight," Grandpa said.

"Your turn to wash dishes," Mom said to me.

"When is the dishwasher getting fixed?" I complained. It had been broken for three months.

"You'll be the first to know," Mom said with a wink. "Now hop to it."

I washed dishes.

"And hey, make yourself useful and get me a cup of coffee," Grandpa said.

I got him coffee.

"Wayne, there's a video on the computer back there in the office," Grandpa said. "I want you to watch it."

"Why?"

"Why must you always ask why?" Grandpa said, irritated. "Just go look at it and you'll understand why."

I watched the video. A video featuring a soldier's funeral at Arlington National Cemetery. The funeral itself made the hairs on the back of my neck stand up.

And I didn't even know the deceased soldier. I watched it again. The way the American flag was draped over the casket, then folded to perfection. Folded thirteen times and tucked in before it took the appearance of a cocked hat. That shape is meant to remind us of the soldiers who served under General George Washington.

I'd looked it up.

The next week, I was still thinking about that video. Still considering ways I could be useful to my family. It struck me like a flash. Something for the Wall of Honor. Something for Uncle Reed. And Mom and Grandpa. My contribution. I watched the video of the service at Arlington National Cemetery again. The flag. Something for Uncle Reed's honor flag. So I found out where I could buy a display shelf that would hold an official honor burial flag with the dimensions five feet by nine and a half feet.

Yeah, I'd looked that up, too.

I found it. A triangular display shelf made of cherry wood. We'd all stare at the Wall of Honor together with Uncle Reed's picture and honor flag. It was one small thing. The last thing I could do for Uncle Reed. I didn't know if it would make Mom feel less sad. But it was better than doing nothing.

There was a small waiting list for the flag case, too. I

ordered it anyway. In fact, right at the second I clicked on *Confirm Your Order*, Grandpa hollered at me.

"Wayne, can you come to the kitchen?"

Mom was standing by the stove, rubbing her chin.

"The date is set. Next weekend," Grandpa said. He put both hands palm-down on the table.

Mom went back to washing a dish she'd already washed.

The doorbell rang. We all froze as if more bad news might be on our doorstep. It wasn't bad news, though. It was Sandy Showalter. Which was really good news!

There she was. So happy. So pretty. So in my house.

"*Hola*, Señor Kovok. Poinsettia delivery!" she said.

Poinsettias.

New topic.

"Sandy, did you know that the red poinsettia originated in Mexico and is named after Joel Roberts Poinsett, the first United States minister to Mexico?"

"Uh, no, I didn't know that, Wayne."

Don't say Frankenbuckettia! Don't say Frankenbuckettia!

"So, if you think about it, that's lucky, because what if his last name was Frankenbucket? Then at Christmas everyone would have to say, *Here, I brought you this Frankenbuckettia.*"

Sandy shoved the four plants into my arms. "You are

29

so funny, Wayne. I told my dad that chicken fact. See you tomorrow."

"Bye." I closed the door and watched her get into her mom's silver minivan. I turned around to face Grandpa.

"Well, Buttercup, you certainly made a square impression on her."

"Whatever," I said. I shoved a poinsettia into his hands.

"What's this?"

"It's a plant. A poinsettia I bought for . . . Never mind."

"I'm going home," Grandpa said, frowning. "I'll arrange the tickets. We leave on Friday. Pack your good suit. Take care of your mother. No complaining about dishes. Hard work never hurt anyone."

"Yes, sir."

On Friday, we flew nonstop to Washington, DC. Our return trip back to Texas would take two flights.

The first of the two, fine. No problems.

CHAPTER 5

It was the last flight that tried to kill us. Just Mom and me.

After the funeral, Grandpa decided to rent a car and drive back to Texas to clear his head. The day went so fast that he forgot to carry Uncle Reed's honor flag with him.

Mom read a magazine. I had a paperback of Steve Jobs's biography. I tried to read the words on the pages, but they wouldn't stick. I had to reread every paragraph. The flag was secure in my lap. It distracted me. I was so curious about its folds. It was so perfect. I wished we were driving with Grandpa. How far had he driven? I wondered. When would he get to Texas? I hadn't even thought to ask him.

The brown-sweatered woman across the aisle from me in 14A tried to get me to talk about Christmas and did

I like the quilt she was making. It was just blocks of red and green. I'd made more creative patterns in Minecraft. I think she said it was a tree skirt. I don't know. My mind couldn't settle on anything. I couldn't even decide if I wanted a snack when the flight attendant offered me one.

"What a day, right?" Mom asked, her eyes all red and glassy.

I nodded. The flag case was on its way to Cedar Drive. I thought about telling her that, but I wanted it to be a surprise. I wanted to wait and see her happy smile as I handed her the case. Maybe it would happen on a spaghetti Tuesday.

"How's your book?" she asked.

"Steve Jobs named his company Apple because it came before Atari in the phone book," I said.

"I thought maybe he just liked apples," she said.

I was going to say that it was true. Steve Jobs did like apples.

But then it sounded like a bomb went off. My ears rang.

At first, it was the plunging feeling when you drop from the highest point of a roller coaster. Only it was worse because I knew it wasn't a ride. I didn't know when the falling would stop. And I knew there was Texas ground below us.

We just kept falling.

Falling, with wind whistling and roaring past my head for a short eternity, only to bounce my head against the seat in front of me. I coughed, spit, and strained for a breath.

Mom, terrified. Me, helpless.

I looked toward the back of the plane.

Something in the back had broken free, leaving a giant hole in the fuselage.

I could see the open sky. I could feel the wind and the rain.

Inside the plane.

And a huge whistling and sucking sound. Objects flying toward the back.

Then there was the screaming. A lot of screaming. And not the roller-coaster kind of screaming. The woman in 14A had a scream to break glass.

Mom gripped the armrest of her seat with one hand. She reached for my hand, too.

"Say a prayer, sweetie," she said to me. "Say something to God. Anything."

I couldn't think of a prayer. Grandpa's voice thundered in my head.

Take care of your mother.

Through the screams, I heard some prayers I might

have borrowed. *Holy Mother, save us. Tell David I love him.* I didn't want to pray. I just waited for God to show up without even asking.

Maybe that was my prayer. I don't know. Does it still count if you thought it but didn't say it out loud?

Then the plane turned hard to the left. Luggage crashed down on us from the overhead bins to the right. A laptop flew toward me like a Frisbee. It slammed into my throat. It made me cough and choke.

The woman in 14A stopped screaming. I looked at her terrified face. The oxygen masks had just dropped down, and she struggled with hers.

Mom said, "Tell me something new, Wayne," which she's said to me a million times in my life.

So I turned to her and even though it hurt to speak, I said, "Did you know that the chameleon has a tongue that is one and a half times the length of its body?"

And I sort of screamed it because that's what you have to do when your plane is going to crash. Paper and screaming and loud prayers and falling oxygen masks are spinning all around you, and your mother is squeezing your hand even harder now and it is turning white under her crazy-strong grip that she must have inherited from generations of Daltons. And it was the weirdest thing, saying a chameleon fact to her as we plummeted.

A flight attendant spoke over the intercom: "For safety reasons, remove your shoes, your glasses, and any pens or items in your pockets."

I automatically put my hand to my head to remove my glasses. They weren't there. I'd started wearing contacts since the fall social. For Sandy. *You have pretty blue eyes, Wayne,* she'd said. I'd said adios to my glasses the next day.

The captain spoke then. "We've experienced a technical difficulty and are preparing for an emergency landing."

His voice was so calm. Too calm.

The beverage cart rolled down the aisle and crashed into the back. Sharp objects hurtled through the air. My face stung as random pieces of people's lives cut into it.

Flight attendants were shouting, "Brace! Brace! Brace!"

We held tight to the seat backs in front of us.

Thoughts swirled about chameleon tongues and the fact that it was a really inconvenient time to die since I finally felt comfortable around Sandy Showalter. Will she cry when I'm gone? What will it feel like when this roller-coaster ride stops? When we land emergently? I thought of our dog, Mr. Darcy. I thought he'd be sad if we didn't come back. He slept by my bed every night.

Turbulence shook the plane. It felt like we'd hit a speed bump and come crashing down onto something hard and solid.

The wind fought with everything. Mom's long brown hair was flying around her face. Papers and books and foam cups and nameless things trailed up and exited the plane. And the flag, too. It had lifted up from my lap, and I grabbed for it by the corner. But that made a corner come untucked. It was tug-of-war. Me versus the wind. The wind was winning.

Mom unbuckled her seat belt to reach after it.

"Mom! No!" I let go of the flag's corner, grabbed her by the waist, pinned her back to her seat.

But the flag got away. It unfurled and sailed up into the fuselage like a patriotic kite before disappearing out the hungry hole.

"Oh, no. Reed!" Mom shouted.

My book fluttered into the wind next. The book took flight like a bird made of pages. And then 14A's red-and-green tree skirt. It went out, too.

The wind had taken everything from us.

It all looked terrifying and beautiful.

All the lights inside the plane blinked once and went out. It was dark as the inside of a pocket.

I think I shouted "Steve!" toward my book.

The flight attendant kept yelling, "Remember to place the oxygen masks on your face and then continue to breathe normally."

Continue to breathe normally?

The plane seemed to level out then. I wondered, was the pilot wrestling with it to stay horizontal? His voice came over the intercom. "Prepare for impact. Prepare for impact!"

How do you prepare for impact? How?

I held my breath. I held on to the seat. Fear was bouncing off everyone.

And then…

Screams.

Crash.

Impact.

Bounce.

> Slide.

> > Slide.

> > > Slide.

Silence.

Smoke.

So much smoke.

Fuel.

Screams.

Heat.

Flickering light.

And then everything came to a dark and silent stop. No one said or did anything. We waited to see if we were alive. We waited for everything to make sense. There was one random thought that rose to the top of my brain. Some fact from Uncle Reed. IED explosions. Accidents. What had he said?

The first ninety seconds after an accident are crucial. It's all about ninety seconds. Don't panic.

So while everyone around me began to move, scream, moan, and panic, I tried to survive.

"Mom!" I screamed over the chaos and smoke. The sharp smell of fuel crept up my neck. I figured we had used up about thirty of the ninety survival seconds. I screamed again and realized no sound was coming from my mouth. No sound at all. Just a hot stab of pain as if a knife were pushing into my throat.

So I grabbed her by the arm, and it made her scream in pain. I pulled her along anyway. I felt my way down the aisle. Other passengers did, too. We'd landed sideways, so walking was difficult. Still, I pulled us toward the gaping hole where rain and moonlight flooded the fuselage. The hole was big and square, like a whole panel of the plane had been cut away. There was a jagged ledge and we stood on it and looked down at the blackness. It was hard to judge how far it was to the ground. Then I heard the terrible sound. The sound of running water. Only it wasn't water. It was jet fuel. So I looked at Mom and I could tell we had the exact same idea. There was no time to stop and calculate or consider the fall. We just had to do it. We held hands and leapt into the darkness. We landed on soft, muddy earth. She screamed.

"Wayne, are you okay? I think I twisted my ankle," Mom said. "I don't know if I can walk."

Maybe sixty of the ninety seconds had passed by then.

I could see orange flames crawling over the plane. My body was stuck in the rain-soaked ground. More passengers landed on the ground near us. I clawed at the damp dirt and tried to pry myself from the muck. Mad because I shouted for help to the few other passengers zombie-walking and crawling across the smoky field. They didn't notice me. Panic rose up through me again. What if the plane went up in a fireball?

Don't panic.

The red lights of emergency vehicles sprayed across the field. I knew we needed to move away from the trickling sound. The smell of jet fuel. Toward those lights. But we were stuck and running out of seconds.

CHAPTER 6

The day after, I startled awake, and for a second I didn't know where I was. If you ask me, waking up in a strange room is almost as scary as a plane crash.

Almost.

I was a plane-crash survivor. A stranger in the new country called AFTER. I was in a hospital bed looking at a tiled ceiling. We'd really crashed, I thought. We'd really leapt from a hole in the plane. The awful smell of jet fuel and mud was still all around me. And the inside of my head was like the inside of our plane. Random stuff bouncing all over the place.

"Rise and shine and pee. It's the best part of waking up, honey," someone said. "It means you're alive. I'm

Nurse Davis. You're in the hospital. You've been in an accident. Your mother is okay. She will be here shortly. You should not try to speak. Your neck suffered a severe blow. Nod your head if you understand."

I nodded. It was the moment I realized that I would have to learn a new language in the country of AFTER.

I opened my mouth to speak anyway. All that came out was a dry gasp. The pain in my throat was sharp and sudden. It made my eyes water.

"Easy now, son," Nurse Davis said.

I'd gotten to the emergency lights and away from the fuel. But I couldn't remember how.

Uncle Reed would've laughed if I told him I was like the crocodile in his story.

Hey, have I got a story for you.

"Don't try to talk now, son," Nurse Davis said.

Do you know how hard that is?

I mean, if you were to try to tell a really funny joke at school, it would be something like this: *Did you know that Wayne Kovok can't talk?*

And everyone would laugh and say, *Yeah, when pigs fly.*

A nurse wheeled Mom up next to me. Her arm was in a giant brace, and she had big bandages on her forehead and right ankle. She pulled herself up onto my bed and hugged me tight.

A doctor with a clipboard came in next.

"Wayne, I'm okay, honey. We're okay," Mom said. "I busted my arm in three places, but I'm fine, okay?"

She didn't look fine.

"No need to worry, Wayne," the doctor explained. "We've got to take a closer look at your neck, though. Some trauma there. You can't talk now because of the swelling. And you had significant cuts on your face, which we stitched up last night. Nod if you understand."

I nodded. Then raised my hand to my face. I could feel a long line of bumpy stitches. They seemed to go on forever, like train tracks starting at the top of my head and traveling across my chin.

"It's okay, Wayne," Mom said. "You still look handsome."

"Wayne, I explained to your mother that the hollow space below your throat is called the suprasternal notch," the doctor said. "It's severely bruised. You may have bowed your vocal cords. We're hopeful it's just a matter of allowing the swelling to go down, but you need to refrain from speaking or eating solid foods for a time."

My suprasternal notch hurt. A lot. The worst pain I could remember. But we'd made it. We'd leapt to our survival. We'd gotten unstuck. There was still mud under my fingernails.

Nurse Davis said, "Okay, we need to give him a moment to go to the restroom."

They all cleared out. I stepped into the tiny bathroom. My ankle gave me a painful reminder. It was sprained but still worked.

First thing I saw in the mirror was that my left eyebrow was missing. My chin was purple, and my neck was red and swollen. Stitches formed a clean zipper line from my forehead, through my shaved left eyebrow, down my cheek, and then across my chin from left to right.

Do you know what it looked like to me?

An L shape.

An L shape of stitches across my face.

The sign of a loser.

It was so pathetic and so Wayne Kovok. I laughed. But you have to use your suprasternal notch to laugh, and when I did, the fire pain shot through me ten times worse than before.

I didn't look so hot before my makeover. And now? A nonverbal Frankenface? Every girl's dream.

Another wave of memory hit me.

The flight. The hole in the fuselage. The things on the plane being sucked out one at a time.

My laptop computer.

Luggage.

Purses.

A one-pound book about Steve Jobs.

A red-and-green quilted Christmas tree skirt from the woman in 14A.

And one precisely folded burial flag presented "from a grateful nation."

Why did this happen? This wasn't the plan.

This was the plan: Fly 179 miles to Dallas. Five hundred miles an hour. A thirty-seven-minute flight. Get home. Unpack. Take dog for a walk. Display flag on Wall of Honor. Call Sandy. Apologize for Frankenbuckettia joke.

A knock on my door. "Honey, you can ring that buzzer in there if you need my help," Nurse Davis said.

I took another glance in the bathroom mirror. I swallowed hard, which also hurt. Then I crawled back into my hospital bed and pulled the sheet over my head.

New topic.

Did you know that for the average lightbulb, only 10 percent of the electricity is turned into light? Ninety percent of the electricity is wasted as heat. Anyway, a flickering lightbulb is annoying. It can flicker right through the sheet covering your head.

So I gave up hiding and tried to watch TV. I clicked through the channels. Soap opera. Soap opera. Spanish

47

soap opera. Lots of good-looking people with good-looking faces.

Bueno.

I finally found *Jeopardy!*

Alex Trebek's favorite *Jeopardy!* category is geography. I don't know why I know that fact, but I do.

I watched *Jeopardy!* and knew all the answers. But I couldn't answer before the contestant did, because my voice was trapped.

No contestant knew the origin of the term *rookie.* I did. It was an American military term coined during the Civil War. Back then, there were so many new recruits pushed into battle without training. The older soldiers called the new recruits "reckies," and it eventually became *rookies.* Grandpa had told me this fact.

Nurse Davis forgot to refill my ice water twice. She apologized and said she was new.

Nurse Rookie.

Grandpa stepped in as Nurse Rookie left. He pushed Mom's wheelchair up to my bed.

He wore the exact same set of clothes he'd had on the last time I saw him. Flannel shirt. Light-blue grandpa jeans. Brown boots. It took my brain a second to remember that he hadn't been on our flight.

My eyes got wide when I saw him. Dark circles underlined his eyes. His face was pale. He needed a shave. My whole life, I'd never seen him without a shaved face.

I sat up and then remembered my backless gown. You can imagine what it feels like to be in front of your grandfather in a flimsy gown.

Grandpa studied me like I was a whole new kind of person. A whole new species.

Don't call me Buttercup. Don't call me Buttercup.

"At ease, son. No waterworks."

"A pen and paper for you," Mom said, handing me a small notepad. "This is how you'll communicate for a while, okay? It'll be fun."

Her voice cracked. Her smile was forced. This was how she acted when she wanted things to seem fine and happy.

"I can teach you some snappy hand signals while you're mute," Grandpa said.

"Dad, he's not mute—he just injured his throat," she said.

"What's the difference?"

"It's a big difference!"

"Anyway, hand signals are widely used in tactical military situations, Wayne," Grandpa said. "Thumbs-up. Thumbs-down. A-OK. Peace. *Digitus impudicus.*"

"What are you talking about?" Mom asked.

"Latin for the aviary gesture. You know, the bir—"

"Dad, I know the aviary gesture!" Mom said. "But he doesn't."

She elbowed him with her non-injured arm. I knew the aviary gesture, all right. You don't get to be in seventh grade without a general knowledge of the dark side.

I used the stupid notepad: How did you get here???

And then I poked him in the arm and handed him the note.

"Caught a flight from Nashville," Grandpa answered.

So my grandfather caught a flight to a plane crash?

Yeah, he caught a flight to a plane crash.

If you ask me, that's braver than the first man who ate an oyster!

I wished I could say that out loud. Mom's face might have a real smile, then.

"Wayne, there's a counselor from the airline here today, but since you can't talk, we'll try that another time, okay?" Mom said. She touched my hair. The fake-happy smile came back.

"And there's a bunch of gosh-darn airline lawyers, too. Talking about signing papers already. Did you hear them?" Grandpa said.

Counselors, I could understand. But airline lawyers sounded funny. So I wrote on my notepad.

Why lawyers?

"Well, um... for the victims, I guess," Mom s.

I wrote: *What victims?*

Mom's face closed up.

That was how I found out about 14A. She had died. She sat one seat across from me in her brown sweater, trying to get me to talk about the red-and-green tree skirt.

It didn't seem possible that two people on the same plane, in the same row, only inches apart, wouldn't both survive. Or both die.

A million questions lined up in my mind. In my lap, I had the writing pad and pen Mom had given me. They looked useless. I was powerless without my voice.

I just wrote: *Why? How?*

She shook her head.

Mom and Grandpa sat by my bed, drinking coffee. They talked like I wasn't even there. It got so I didn't even mind.

Because I was thinking about 14A. How I hadn't talked to her. How I'd ignored her. *Sorry, woman in 14A.*

I swallowed hard. And that ignited all the pain in my neck again. I kept hurting myself.

Just then, my dad rounded the corner into my hospital room. I was on the brink of waterworks. I stared at a plant on the table. I filled my eyes with green so that they wouldn't fill with anything else.

Green, green, green!

"Hey there," he said. "You okay?"

"We'll give you two a minute," Mom said. She and Grandpa left the room.

My dad fixed me with a worried look, squinting really. Kind of like the way Grandpa first scanned me. You can imagine how it feels to have the people you've known your whole life look at you like you're a stranger from a strange land. My dad seemed jittery. I don't know if I'd ever seen him worried. He put something on my table and then stuffed his hands in his pockets.

"I didn't know what to get you," he said. "It's stupid." It was a teddy bear. It had the words GET WELL on its stupid T-shirt.

No, it's okay.

"Man, what you guys went through," he said. "I'd say you're lucky to be alive!"

They kept telling me to nod if I understood, so I nodded, pretending to understand. I was alive. But I didn't feel lucky. Maybe that would come later. Now it was burst after burst of confusion. Because what were the facts about the crash? Why had it happened? Why didn't everyone survive?

"So, you can't talk?"

I nodded again. His nervousness was making me nervous.

"Hey, I heard Imagine Dragons are going to be in town next week," he said. "You like them, right? We could go!"

I tried my best to smile and nod yes.

"Say, did you know someone in the hall said your mother unbuckled her seat belt in the plane? Is that true?"

So I took my notepad and wrote: *To get Uncle Reed. Burial flag.*

"Is that so?" the Flee said. "Just for a flag?"

It was my fault she did it. I wasn't stronger than the wind.

On the flight to Arlington, Grandpa had explained that burial flags have covered fallen soldiers since the Napoleonic Wars. I remembered that.

The American burial flag is draped so that the stars are over the left shoulder of the soldier, he'd said.

I wrote these facts on my notepad and gave them to my dad.

"But you're okay now," he said. "That's what's important. I'm glad you're okay." He put a hand on my foot. Which was as awkward as it sounds. But my dad was never a hugger.

"Okay, get some rest, son," he said. "Maybe you could ride back to town with me, huh? The doctor said you'll be released tomorrow. How would you like that?"

I shrugged.

"Okay, see you," he said.

I tried to settle my mind. Every time I dozed off, I had that falling feeling. Heard the flight attendants shouting, *Brace!*

I turned the TV back on, and a guy named Tim LeMoot, the Texas Boot, shouted from the screen.

Here's the thing: LeMoot was legendary in Texas for his screaming commercials.

He shouted from the TV, "HURT IN AN ACCIDENT? CALL ME *NOW*! I'LL KICK CASH RIGHT INTO YOUR WALLET! I'LL GET WHAT YOU DESERVE! CALL ME *NOW*! I'M WAITING!"

Have you ever met someone who can only talk in caps?

Tim LeMoot's voice had one volume: ALL CAPS!

Man, he *really* wanted you to call him.

You had to wonder if that was how he sounded in real life. Maybe he stood at the deli counter and placed his order in ALL CAPS.

I'D LIKE A POUND OF SLICED SMOKED TUR-KEY RIGHT NOW! I'M WAITING!

Sandy Showalter would think that was a funny joke. I'd remember it for her later.

And then all I could think about was Tim LeMoot,

the Texas Boot, because what if someone really was in an accident and wanted to call him, but his face and throat were all beat up and he couldn't? And it was because of a flag, but not just any flag?

And what did you do when you wanted to say a lot of words? A lot of words about flags and phone calls and survivors and victims, but you couldn't speak? What did you do then, Tim LeMoot, the Texas Boot? And why did this all happen in the first place?

Why? Why? Why?

There it was again. The question why. The plaguing question. Just as Uncle Reed had told me.

I was plagued for sure.

CHAPTER 7

Late the next afternoon, when *Jeopardy!* was over and *Judge Judy* was coming on TV in ten minutes, we were told we could leave the hospital. They called us the "treated and released" survivors. There was another group still in the hospital. Hospital attendants wheeled me and Mom outside, where Grandpa sat in the front seat of a rental car. Reporters shouted questions at us. Camera flashes went off. Another of the treated-and-released group agreed to speak to the reporters.

I hadn't expected all that. I'd expected to just drive off with my dad.

I passed Mom a note.

Dad???

"Oh, he had to get back home and said to tell you

he was sorry," she said. "He said he'd try to call you this week."

My dad. The Flee. He liked to drive at top speed with rock music at top volume. I'd been looking forward to that for my getaway from the hospital. Grandpa's driving? It would be the opposite. Exact speed limit and talk radio.

True story.

Well, it was my fault. I'd only shrugged when he asked me if I wanted to ride home with him. I could have nodded yes. I should have written a note. Why didn't I write a note?

We rode home inside the rental car, which smelled of old cheese. Miles passed on the road. Rain poured down until the terrain changed from thick pine trees to flat, cold nothing. Grandpa hummed along to country music, which was worse than talk radio, and Mom checked her messages.

"Oh, Wayne, there's a call from Sandy," she said. "How nice. She hopes you're feeling better. And, honey, just so you're prepared, the crash has been all over the news."

Do you want to know something? My whole life, I had dreamed I'd be in the news for some big achievement. Not a tragedy.

Mom and Grandpa talked quietly. I tried to sleep but kept jerking awake. The sensation of falling seemed to hit me every time I dozed off. I'd suddenly feel as if I were inside the plane again. Maybe this was what it was like to survive a plane crash. Maybe that falling feeling was here to stay.

I tried to stay awake so that I wouldn't fall. I caught bits of front-seat conversation.

"I just can't believe we couldn't hold on to the flag, Dad," Mom said.

"You were holding on for dear life, honey," Grandpa answered.

"It was so frightening," she said.

"And you lived!" Grandpa patted her hand. Mom wore her sad face.

"I don't even know what happened. Everything went so fast. So terribly fast."

"Now, Jennifer, you always draw the best bull. Not to worry now that you're on solid ground," he said. I'd heard this a million times. This was Grandpa-speak for *Don't worry.*

Grandpa turned the car onto Cedar Drive. Looking at the street, I got the funniest feeling. It was like I'd been gone for a month. As if it were a different season. As if my old street had changed while I was away.

When I got inside the house, I got the same feeling. The house seemed smaller. I didn't look at the perfect wall. I rushed into my room and closed the door.

Somehow, my room was the same as it had always been. Except there were three dried-out poinsettia plants on my desk. A few fallen, dead leaves on my floor.

I pictured them screaming to me in the voice of Tim LeMoot, the Texas Boot.

WE NEED WATER NOW! WE'RE WAITING!

Oh, you're thirsty? Well, I almost died on the way home from a funeral. Sorry, plants.

I flopped onto my bed. I was so tired. I slapped my hand across my forehead.

That hurt.

I forgot how many stitches were up there.

It felt like there were more stitches than skin.

In the shape of an L.

That I got because I was in a plane crash.

Where was all the news about the crash? Did they know what had happened? I had to do research. Mom and Grandpa wouldn't answer my questions. I'd tossed at least ten written questions into the front seat of the rental car. Mom replied to every one of the notes with the same answer: *Don't worry about that now, Wayne.*

When was the best time to worry? Later?

Well, now it was later, and I wasn't so much worried as I was curious.

So when Mom napped and Grandpa left to pick up

Mr. Darcy from Bone Jour, the pet boarding place, I searched for information on the computer in our guest room.

The first thing I viewed on the Internet was a picture of the Flight 56 wreckage. An aerial photo showed a dark, half-mile-long gash where the plane had skidded into the earth before stopping in a row of pine trees. The pine trees nearest the crash were blackened. The plane itself looked charred and muddy. You could make out the rip in the side of the plane where the rain had come in and our things had gone out.

I'd guessed right. The pilot had regained some control. He'd been able to level the plane out so that it slid instead of doing a nosedive. Experts said the pilot's experience saved lives. The article said that the National Transportation Safety Board was going to investigate and reconstruct the plane. The black boxes were intact. Weather was thought to be a factor. Twelve of the forty-four passengers had died, including the experienced pilot. Another dead hero.

New Internet search.

Did you know the landing tires on an airplane are filled with nitrogen, not air? Nitrogen is less susceptible to volume changes than regular air, and it's also an inert gas, making it less flammable.

Did you know that when a plane crashes and the accident is called in, emergency responders ask, *How many souls on board?* They use the word *souls* to identify all people on the aircraft, not just passengers. It's a holdover from the days when people traveled at sea.

Did you know that *Mayday* is an international distress signal? It's translated from the French term *m'aidez*, which means "come help me."

That's a pretty good distress call for any situation, from seventh graders plummeting from the sky to guys stuck next to Sandy Showalter at the Beatty Middle School fall social who have run out of solid things to say.

Mayday.

Come help me.

My lips formed the word.

Mayday. Mayday. Mayday.

I went back to my room and sat on the bed. My body felt tired and heavy, and I finally fell asleep. I woke up when Mr. Darcy jumped onto my bed.

"I'm back with your mutt," Grandpa shouted.

I sat up in bed and hugged Mr. Darcy.

I was so happy to see my dog. I wanted to talk to my dog. I hugged his head and tried to press some thoughts into him.

It's okay, boy. I fell out of the sky.

Do you know what? He seemed to understand.

I like that about Mr. Darcy.

I came out of my room, wiping dog drool from my face.

"Put that in the guest room and don't wake up your mother," Grandpa said, pointing to a duffel bag. Then he sat down in the one big, comfy chair we have in our living room. That chair is uniquely positioned for optimum TV watching.

Do you know how I knew that? Because I had uniquely positioned it there for my own TV viewing. Next to the chair, there is a fluffy, flowery sofa, which I don't like to sit on because it's so girly. Epically girly. But Mom loves it. On the day it was delivered, I thought maybe she loved it the way she loved the Wall of Honor.

Look, Wayne, this is my first-ever piece of adult furniture, she'd said. In our last house with my dad, we had a futon and a rocking chair.

Grandpa was still sitting in the big chair.

"Hey, Wayne, if you're going to the kitchen, would you bring me that sandwich that's in the fridge?" he asked.

I got the sandwich for Grandpa to eat. It was starting to seem like this was *his* house. He'd spread out his shaving kit on the bathroom counter. He'd folded a laundry load of towels into precise squares. He'd even plugged in the small, fake Christmas tree.

"You'll like this TV show, Wayne," he said. "Oh, I put a little silver bell next to your mother's table. Listen for that in case she needs anything."

The bell was a good idea. Mom's arm was still in a brace. Her twisted ankle was better but still sore. So Mom could ring for us like the English maids she loved to watch on TV. That's all she wants to watch sometimes. Movies where people use fake British accents and run through fields and yell, *Oh, I think I'll run through this field in search of a husband.*

That is a clue about why we have a dog named Mr. Darcy. We got him about the same time as the flowery sofa, which I don't think was a coincidence. Mr. Darcy is her favorite character in Jane Austen movies. Nothing would make Mom happier than for Mr. Darcy to go missing so that she could go running out onto Cedar Drive, shouting, *Mr. Darcy, Mr. Darcy! Come home, Mr. Darcy. I've been looking for you everywhere, Mr. Darcy.*

True story.

I could feel a Jane Austen marathon coming on.

Grandpa and I watched a show about military tactics. Grandpa fell asleep in the big chair. I sat on the flowery couch at an angle that was definitely not optimal for TV watching. I found out lightning quick how to wake up Grandpa: Try to steal the TV remote from his hands. He will bolt upright in his chair and ask you what in the name of Sam Hill you are trying to do.

"What in the name of Sam Hill are you trying to do, Wayne?"

Did you know that Sam Hill was an American businessman who liked to swear a lot, so his name became a euphemism for a swearword?

Mr. Darcy snuck a bite of Grandpa's sandwich.

"What in the name of Sam Hill is your dog trying to do, Wayne?" Grandpa leapt from his chair, shooing Mr. Darcy toward me.

I sensed that an invoking-the-name-of-Sam-Hill marathon was coming on, too.

I was trapped between Jane Austen and Sam Hill.

Ding, ding.

I beat Grandpa to Mom's room, not because I'm faster. I am faster. Only he didn't try to race me. He ordered me to do it.

"Can you go do that, Wayne?" he said.

Sure, have the plane-crash victim do everything. You just sit there, Grandpa, and eat your sandwich. But I couldn't say that. Even when I had a voice, I was smart enough to keep my sarcasm to myself around Grandpa. Uncle Reed said that when recruits spouted off to Grandpa during basic training, they had to run with a concrete block until dark.

I'm not saying I'm scared of my grandfather. Okay, maybe a little. But let's just say I never wanted to know if he'd treat his grandson like a snarky recruit.

Mom's room was quiet and dark.

"Come sit with me and we'll watch a movie, okay?" Her hair hung down, curtain-style. The sad face.

A movie marathon of British women with high-pitched voices running through fields looking for husbands was about to happen. I'd totally called it.

All I could hope for was that she'd let me bring a book, and I could read while she watched.

"Wayne, where does your mother keep the coffee filters?" Grandpa shouted from the kitchen. I'd brought him a sandwich. Iced tea. Given up the chair. One more thing. Fine.

"Go help him find the filters, would you, Wayne?" Mom said.

Grrr.

You would think being a fresh, new plane-crash survivor with one hundred stitches in your face would earn a little laziness.

"Show him where everything is in the bathroom, too,"

Mom added. "He's going to need your help now that he'll be moving in."

I wrote on my notepad: What????? Wait, living here? Here?

I couldn't write Why? fast enough.

"It's just temporary until I can drive again. It was either that or have *us* move to his house. Or, would you want that, maybe? To move there?"

I considered this option. Grandpa lived in a small town house. It had two bedrooms. I'd probably have to share with him. Or, weirder, with my mom.

I wrote: No, here is better.

"Okay, give it a chance, Wayne," Mom said. "It's temporary."

I know.

"We missed Christmas." Mom was about to cry.

Did you know scorpions can survive for a year without food or water?

Mom's face changed from sad to sad with a smile. "I love how your mind works, Wayne."

I went into the kitchen and pulled down the box of coffee filters.

"Thanks," Grandpa said. I watched him heap scoop after scoop of coffee into a coffee filter. I paid attention to how he made his coffee. Because it probably wouldn't be long before I'd hear, *Wayne, go make me some coffee*.

I rearranged Mom's collection of blue glass birds on the kitchen counter. Someone (Grandpa) had placed them in rows. Mom liked them in a circle.

Grandpa poured himself a steaming cup of coffee, then leaned against the counter.

"So, Wayne, that flag, huh?" he said. "Darn shame, that flag." His face was so full of new wrinkles.

I nodded. Do you know what it feels like to be a human bobblehead? Well, I did. In the past twenty-four hours, I'd nodded more than I had my entire life.

I was starting to get the feeling that since the volume of my voice was muted, it had turned up inside my head. It was really loud in there. Facts that I couldn't say stood at the ready. Facts that could fill up an uncomfortable silence like the one I was having with Grandpa. Statements I couldn't make about honor flags weighing around four pounds and being made of cotton.

I'd looked it up.

I stared at the linoleum floor and told my brain to shut up and wait for the appropriate time to bolt out of the kitchen.

"I have a flag your great-grandfather once owned,"

Grandpa said. "Reed really liked that flag. You know the one I'm talking about? With the wood frame and glass case?"

Yeah, I knew the one. That was where I'd gotten the idea for Uncle Reed's display case, which, as a matter of fact, had been on our porch when we got home. It remained unopened inside its cardboard box, stuffed in my closet. No one knew about it but me and the mailman. When the flag was found, I would fill it and present it to Mom and Grandpa. I, Wayne Kovok, the guy who let go of the flag, would set everything straight. No one would remember that I couldn't hold on to it. That was the plan.

"I just can't figure it," Grandpa said. "The whole crash. Reed."

His face went sad, remembering.

Did you know that the word *linoleum* is derived from the Latin *linum*, which means "flax," and *oleum*, which means "oil"? This is because a main ingredient in linoleum is linseed oil, and will you please stop talking about a flag that couldn't possibly have been saved from being sucked out of the plane?

"You know, you're probably right, Wayne. A four-pound flag against that wicked wind didn't stand a chance," Grandpa said. His voice cracked. "Didn't stand a chance. Maybe when you join the army one day, you'll discover that sometimes it's man versus nature. A man has to be strong."

I didn't know what to say. *(Sorry my skinny little arms couldn't hold on to the flag?)* Grandpa leaned into the countertop. His shoulders shook. Grandpa served in the army for more than thirty years. He was not a crier. This was the first time I'd ever seen him with tears on his face. His eyes had deep lines under them. He didn't look the same anymore. He looked broken.

I'd missed my chance at an exit. I'd stayed there too long, wondering what to do, staring at him.

And then his eyes met mine. In an instant, the drill sergeant was back. It surprised me how glad I was that his tough face had returned.

"Don't you have something useful to do!" he barked.

I got out of there. Fast.

New topic.

The flag was missing. But that just meant it was somewhere else. Waiting to be found or replaced. A hypothesis waiting to be made into a true fact.

An idea for a project swirled inside my beat-up head.

A project to find the flag.

I avoided Mom. I avoided Grandpa.

I began collecting data right away.

I took a chance slipping into the guest room, but I

didn't think Grandpa would come down the hallway. I flipped on the computer and pulled up the articles about the crash. I printed out pages. Authorities were already collecting debris. I taped the data pages inside my closet door, where no one could see. I'd track the news. Monitor the collection of debris. Claim the flag once it was found. Watch the military service videos online and learn how to refold it. Present it to my mom and Grandpa.

Do you know what it felt like?

I'll tell you.

I almost felt useful.

DATA

The American burial flag is made of cotton.

• Dimensions: five feet by nine and a half feet

• Weight: four pounds

Question: Can it be replaced?

Answer: No. The US Department of Veterans Affairs states that the law allows for one burial flag per veteran. It cannot be replaced if it is lost, destroyed, or stolen.

CHAPTER 8

A late-December rain poured down outside. The wind slapped it against my window. I'd pulled up the blinds in my room to watch it at night. Across the street, our neighbors still had a giant white inflatable Christmas snowman in their front yard. The snowman swayed in the wind. Most nights since we got home, I hadn't slept all the way through. I'd had nightmares of falling. I'd wake up from the nightmare right at the moment Mom and I leapt from the plane. It will sound strange, but sometimes I wished I could stay in the nightmare five minutes longer. It might have given me a clue about how we got to the hospital. Because I only remembered the awful stink of jet fuel and then jumping. The fuselage was about twenty feet above the ground when it came to a stop in that field. Twenty feet is about the height of a two-story building.

I'd looked it up.

So we'd leapt twenty feet into the darkness. If it hadn't hurt Mom so much, I might have considered that a cool fact.

But once I knew that fact, I stopped having the jumping nightmare. I didn't know facts could do that.

Several other survivors had also jumped from the wreckage. Those facts had been printed in a recent article and added to my find-the-flag project.

As far as the crash was concerned, the National Transportation Safety Board announced it had collected 70 percent of the plane debris, the black boxes, and a substantial number of items belonging to the passengers, but there was no mention of a missing American flag. The initial findings of the cause of the crash were expected in about six to eight weeks.

Mom had gone to the doctor for a new arm brace.

"Look, Wayne, I'm learning to use my left hand now," she said. She was proud of her progress.

I went to a voice specialist and was evaluated.

"It's going to take some time, Wayne, but you should be talking in three months or less," the doctor said. He was proud of his diagnosis.

And neighbors brought us food that tortured my taste buds. Do you know what it's like to look at delicious food you can't eat? It's like this. It's like looking at the school lunch calendar and counting the days until it's pizza-stick day. Pizza-stick day was a reason to go to school. Seriously. Even parents came to school for lunch on pizza-stick day. They were legendary.

All that food in our fridge? It was like getting in line to purchase pizza sticks only to have the cafeteria lady say, *We just ran out, Wayne. Sorry.*

True story.

The biggest new fact was that Grandpa had *really* moved into our house. He brought four things with him that he was very proud of.

The Car, a.k.a. his pristine 1967 candy apple–red Mustang convertible that "you may never lean against or get near under penalty of death." A beat-up suitcase that "you may never touch." A closetful of button-down flannel shirts that "you may get out of the dryer right now." And Hank Williams. Hank Williams was a red-eared slider turtle who "you'd better feed right now."

Every time Grandpa saw me, he had an order for me to go and do something useful. And it was fine by me. I was trying my best to avoid him. On a scale from one to awkward, we were off the charts.

New topic.

Get-well cards.

Did you know there was a man in New York who received a winning lottery ticket inside a get-well card while he was in the hospital? He did. When he scratched it off, he realized he'd won seven million dollars.

True story.

Our kitchen countertop was littered with cards, some of which included bad poetry. One was from my dad. He wrote that he'd try to stop by soon. My dad was remarried now and had a new little kid. They didn't even live far from us. You would think that would make it easy to stop by. You would think.

"You should go do something with your dad," Mom said.

Why? I was still annoyed about not driving home from the hospital with him. I could have written him a note, but he could have stayed, too.

"Because he's your dad," she said.

So?

"You're being stubborn. It's good to be around him a little bit," she said. "He can teach you man things."

Man things?

"You know what I mean."

No. No, I didn't.

74

So I told her I'd think about it so that she wouldn't get all worked up.

Some other get-well cards declared that every cloud had a silver lining.

The poet John Milton is the originator of this saying.

I looked it up.

Well, I had been *inside* an actual cloud. Its lining was not silver. It was more of a dirty cotton ball. (That is a fact, Mr. Milton.)

This just proved my theory about poets. They are making stuff up so that life will sound better than it is. I didn't know why Sandy was such a fan.

If there was any silver lining in my situation, it was that the plane had crashed during Christmas break. I planned to hide out on Cedar Drive as long as possible.

But the Saturday morning after I'd stayed awake watching the rain through my window, school came to me.

"Wayne," Grandpa called. "Report to the front door. A trio of friends is here to see you."

My mind raced. *A trio?*

There were three kids from Beatty Middle School in my entryway. Their mouths hung open. Eyes fixed on me with the kind of looks people displayed when they drove past a car crash. I'd forget that my face was all beat up, and then someone would look at me and I'd remember all over again.

"Hi, Wayne," Mysti said. She handed me a card. I was sure it was a get-well card.

"Duuuuuude. Your face," Anibal said.

Anibal stretched the word *dude* into two syllables. Rama elbowed him hard in the rib cage.

Coming to my house was probably the idea of Mysti Murphy and Rama Khan. Those two girls had nice ideas, such as letting me sit at their lunch table or sharing delicious pizza sticks.

No way was it shoe-stealing Anibal Gomez's idea. He did *not* have a reputation for having nice ideas. He had a reputation for having ideas only he thought were funny, like stealing my shoes and hiding them in the library.

So the fact that he was involved in coming to Cedar Drive put me on high alert.

"Has Sandy seen you, man?" Anibal said, cocking his head to the right.

"Don't listen to him, Wayne," Rama said. "He's a fetus."

No, Sandy hasn't seen me. Why? What has she told you?

They studied me. Studied me like I was a test and they had to memorize details. The fill-in-the-blank spot where my eyebrow used to live. The L shape of stitches across my face. And also, my new, shorter hair. Mom thought it was a good idea for both of us to shorten our hair. Good idea for her, maybe. I just did it because I was doing whatever she said.

My mouth went dry and then tried to cough up something to say, but all that came out was *Errrr*.

"We brought you something," Mysti said.

She handed me a brown paper sack. It said GOODWILL in red lettering on the outside.

"We brought you shoes," Anibal said, at which point Rama elbowed him a second time. "What? They're shoes. Which is kinda funny coming from me, but that's how we knew your shoe size. Ironic, huh?"

Stupid irony.

"Don't make me regret bringing you with us, Anibal," Mysti said. "Anyway, we heard you lost your shoes, and, well, Anibal *did* know your shoe size."

I didn't lose them. I left them behind.

Do you know why flight attendants tell you to take off your shoes and remove any pens or pencils from your pockets before an emergency landing? This is because the emergency slides are inflatable. They don't want any shoes or pens to puncture the slide on the way down.

I looked it up.

Somewhere in the chaos of the plane's free fall, I'd

followed those instructions. Which turned out to be stupid because there were no slides for our emergency exit.

"Sorry they aren't new shoes," Mysti said. "We couldn't afford much right now."

I couldn't say anything. And then I realized that I didn't want to say anything.

I wanted to disappear.

"Well, my mom is waiting for us in the car," Rama said. "We hope you get better and come back to school soon."

Mysti looked like she might cry. I swallowed hard. I stared at the brown bag. I suddenly wanted them to leave.

I wondered how I could avoid school. Maybe my plane-crash status would free me for the rest of the semester, let me make up my classes during the summer. I would look it up later and check.

I'd seen a reflection of the new Wayne Kovok in their eyes. I didn't like it.

Do you know how to make this look? Okay, just as your dog straight-tails it and takes a dump, glance over at him. You got it? You are repulsed. The dog is humiliated. It's awful for all parties involved.

So that was how Mysti, Rama, and Anibal looked at my face.

With the dog-dump stare.

And *they* were my friends. How would nonfriends look at me?

I opened the Goodwill bag. There was an old, beat-up pair of dingy white tennis shoes. Someone else's shoes.

And they fit perfectly because I was now, in fact, someone else. Someone from another country. Another planet.

I decided right then that I didn't want to see my Beatty Middle School friends. More accurately, I didn't want to be *seen* by them. I wanted to hide. I'd figure out a way.

So I went to our computer and typed out an e-mail before I lost my nerve.

Data sent to Mysti via e-mail because she was the only one safe to tell:

Dear Mysti,

Thanks for the shoes. No offense, but I don't want to be around anyone at all right now. I'm going to go monk for a while. Or maybe I should say go mime, without the stupid striped shirt. I already have the no-voice part down. Explain this to Rama. I'm writing this to you because you know how she is—she will try to convince me I should talk to you guys. I want to be alone now, okay? Please understand.

W

Data received from Mysti via e-mail:

Wayne,

I understand. Once my mother put a bowl on my head and then cut my hair. It was hideous. I wanted to disappear! Rama said to look up emu oil for your face, BTW. Sorry about stupid Anibal.

M

And that was how I said good-bye to my old friends.

And a friend said good-bye to me.

A friend who sort of compared surviving a plane crash to having a horrible haircut.

A friend who took my request for being a middle school monk without any protest.

I mean, I expected a little protest.

A tiny protest.

A crumb of a protest.

Do you know what happened to that crocodile that survived the plane crash in the Congo? I'll tell you what happened because I looked it up. (Uncle Reed left out one very interesting detail about that story.)

The crocodile? It got a machete chop by first responders at the crash site. Yeah. It survived the whole plummet and fall and crash. It survived!

And then it was sliced through the head, dead.

I'm not saying that Mysti's e-mail was the same as a machete chop. No way. I'm saying that plane-crash survivors don't have any special superpowers. They can still get hurt *after* the crash.

True story.

CHAPTER 9

It was New Year's Eve, and I decided the day had to be good.

Good-bye, year that tried to kill me!

That's what I could write on a card. No poetry. All truth.

Wasn't New Year's the time to move forward? Make goals?

Right after lunch, do you know what hit me out of the blue? No, not an idea. A notebook.

A coffee-scented notebook.

"Don't leave your stuff lying around, Wayne," Grandpa said.

Man, the trouble with not being able to talk is that you

can't shoot off a remark to the person throwing things at you. You have to hurry up and write it down, and by then the person has turned his back to you so that he can get more coffee. Not that I would have said or written anything.

I picked up the notebook.

And I guess I stared at the wall thinking about my weird life for longer than a person should stare at a wall. Because Uncle Reed's official army photo was on the Wall of Honor now. I couldn't help but stare at it. The colors in it were so new and bright compared to the other photos.

"Why are you looking at that wall for so long?" Grandpa asked.

Because that's what voiceless people in the country of AFTER do now. They stare at things.

"If you wait any longer, you'll turn thirteen right here in this hallway."

I shrugged. Citizens of this new land also shrug. A lot.

"If this wall could talk, huh?" he said. "What stories these photos, these men would tell."

If this wall could talk? Really? He was more interested in learning the language of a wall than understanding me and the reason I had notebooks all over the house?

I waited him out. Maybe he would tell a patriotic story or order me to go and do a chore. It could have gone either way.

Grandpa took a long sip from his coffee mug. "If you've got time to stare at a wall, you've got time to unload the dryer and fold the clothes."

Do you know what? It went the way I predicted it would.

I did that chore, and then he ordered me to do a new one.

"What you need for your recovery is to stay busy," he said. "That will make you stronger."

I looked at the clock. I was counting the hours until Grandpa left for some appointment. He was going to see a doctor because his back hurt. My back hurt, too.

Hellooooo, I fell out of the sky!

"Son, are you listening?" he asked. "Hank Williams needs to eat at noon."

I wrote: *I know!*

"When are you expected back at school?"

Christmas break!!!

"Oh, going soft, are you?"

Grrrr.

My New Year's attitude was sinking. I was still in my PJs. Maybe I would just go back to bed. Read. Hide.

I wrote on my notepad: *Not soft, G.*

"Who is this G?" Grandpa asked.

You! Grandpa = G.

"Oh, okay, W," Grandpa said.

School. I wasn't going to go back. Not like this. Not with my zippered-up face. Not without a voice full of facts to shield me from awkward situations.

So Grandpa finally left for his appointment and then Mom rang her little bell, and all my hopes for New Year's Eve being good evaporated. I pinned my hopes on the new year itself. What choice did I have?

"Would you bring me an ice pack, honey?" she asked.

I brought her an ice pack. We sat in her room watching the news. Before the crash, I never watched the news. Didn't care at all. But now I got up every day thinking, *This is the day. This is the day the news will say something about the flag.*

A woman named Liz Delaney reported every other day. She'd give an update on passengers newly released from the hospital. Some new fact. Some new piece of debris retrieved. Some amazing story about witnesses in town watching the plane as it came down. An aviation expert giving his opinion on the cause of the crash. All the reports were pretty interesting.

What if today was *the* day?

It wasn't.

Liz Delaney reported that two suitcases had been miraculously found on a roadside with hardly any scratches. She thought it was so miraculous that there was a pristine wrapped Christmas present the size of a cereal box on the roof of a barn. Not a single singe or tear in the paper. The curly red bow still intact.

Liz Delaney concluded her report with, "In addition to finding a seat belt in Fred Haney's goat pen, we've also discovered a copy of the Bible. What do you think of that, Mr. Haney?"

"Well, I always suspected my goats were God-loving mammals."

"It's not confirmed, but this might be further debris from the airline tragedy that occurred two weeks ago. This is Liz Delaney reporting from Marshall, Texas, for KTSB-Three News."

"I guess they have a lot of ground to cover," Mom said. I had the feeling she got up every day expecting to hear news about Uncle Reed's flag. Just like me.

I guess.

"I mean, they have to find it. How hard can it be?"

Pretty hard.

Mom didn't know it, but a couple of days ago, I'd looked up Liz Delaney's e-mail and shot her a message.

Dear Ms. Delaney,

I am a survivor of Flight 56 that crashed near Marshall, Texas. I'm following your newscasts about found objects. I'm searching for my uncle's American flag. Our family received this at his funeral. It's very important to us. I hope you will help. Please write back.

Wayne H. Kovok

Sending the message made me feel like I was doing something. It was a major new step in the right direction. Putting things right on the Wall of Honor.

"You're probably so bored, Wayne, and can't wait to go back to school, huh?" Mom twisted her hair.

Skip school next semester?

"What? I don't know, Wayne."

So I wrote to Mom that I didn't feel like going

87

back to Beatty Middle School. Look at my eyebrow-challenged, stitched-up face if you have questions.

I underlined *eyebrow* three times.

And she reached out to touch my face the way moms can't help doing *ever*, and I flinched because it hurt. Even my pillow hurt my face.

"It's not that bad," she said.

Yes. It. IS. My face is epically unbalanced. Eyebrows are important!

She eased off the bed with her one good arm and went into her bathroom for a few minutes. She returned to her bed and smiled at me. She'd shaved off her perfectly good left eyebrow! Shaved it clean off for no good reason. I raised my right eyebrow.

Wait, what? Why did you do that?

"See, it doesn't look as strange as you think it does."

But it did. It did look strange. God gave us two eyebrows for a reason. Balance. Symmetry. Expression.

Why?

"It's solidarity. We will heal and grow eyebrows together," she said. "Now, eventually you have to go to school just like I have to go back to work. I'm not saying it'll be easy, but we have to move forward."

I nodded.

"You've given me an idea," she said, typing fast on her

laptop. She could type pretty fast for someone with a big brace down one arm.

"There. I have a friend whose daughter goes to this school." She pointed to her computer screen. The West Academy. A school for star athletes, actors, or special students who went to school for half the day and trained, acted, or were otherwise special for the other half.

"What do you think? I bet we could get you in there. Half days, too. New friends."

Can we afford it?

"Leave that up to me," she said. "The airline is going to settle with the passengers, so I think we'd be covered." We'd gone months without a new dishwasher. And I wanted to replace my lost laptop. A private school seemed like a stretch.

I couldn't stop staring at the space on her face that had once had a perfect eyebrow. The skin was really white where her eyebrow had been. Who messed up their face on purpose? I forced myself to stop staring. I looked at the school where I could be considered special for no good reason.

It made sense to be in a place where no one knew me. Keep my head down. No expectations. No history. No friends. The idea had promise.

Mom cried.

Okay. Okay. I'll go to school.

"It's not that."

Your eyebrow?

"No. Never mind. I'm fine. I don't know what's wrong with me."

Quickly, I wrote her a note.

Did you know that there's a guy in Australia who collected his own belly button lint for more than twenty years? He had three jars of it.

It wasn't exactly a dazzling fact.

"You *definitely* need to go back to school."

You need a new eyebrow!

"It's temporary."

Why were you crying?

"I don't know. I get sad in waves. I guess a wave hit me."

Sorry.

A few hours later, I was invited to a party. Okay, I was invited to a party by my dad, who rarely invited me to anything. Mom said I should go, listen to music, try to have fun. It's hard to argue the definition of fun with a sad, one-browed parent. So I agreed to go.

He said he'd be here at nine.

I stood at the kitchen window, waiting for his car to roll up. Five minutes after nine.

Be on time. Be on time!

It was ten minutes after nine and still nothing. But so what. What's ten minutes?

Grandpa hovered behind me. Waiting for my dad to be late. I knew it. He didn't like my dad. I once overheard him saying my dad had the backbone of an éclair. I'm pretty sure he was the one who'd started calling him the Flee.

"You want a ride over there?" Grandpa asked.

Nope.

I couldn't look at him. I was afraid my face would show my thoughts. Grandpa didn't think my dad was going to show up anytime soon. I was starting to doubt it, too.

Please, be on time! Be on time! Don't make me look stupid!

"Being on time is a virtue," Grandpa said.

My nerves rattled me and I started to sweat. Like it was my fault Dad was late. I wished Grandpa knew that I was allergic to being tardy. My teachers always said so.

Dad showed up ten minutes later. Only twenty minutes late. I grabbed my jacket and hustled toward the front door, smiling. Smiling with so much relief that it pulled at my stitches and made my face feel tight.

"He's bringing you home, right?" Grandpa asked. I

nodded yes, still smiling. "Well, call if anything changes. If you need help."

I wasn't going to need help. My dad had said he'd be there and he was. I raced down the front walk, excited about the party, the new year. Everything.

CHAPTER 10

Well, I didn't need to be so excited.

"We invited a few friends and neighbors," Dad said as he opened the front door to his house. There were black and gold balloons everywhere. Plates and cups on the coffee table and every other table in the place. The smell of pizza and grilled chicken. My mouth watered. My stomach growled.

"Do you want something to eat?" he asked.

I started to write something on my notepad about not eating solid foods, but I stopped because I'd just noticed his shirt. It was an Imagine Dragons T-shirt.

I pointed to his shirt and wrote him a note: Did you go to the concert?

"Oh, yeah, it was great," he said, smiling. "We ended up with only two tickets. Next time you can go, okay?"

Next thing I knew, my dad had his arm around my shoulders. Like I was a good friend. Like he was glad I was there.

"Hey, everyone," he shouted above the music. "This is my son! He survived that plane crash and is here in one piece. How about that?"

His friends cheered.

"He's the big man now! He can fly," he said, his arm still around me. His friends laughing.

It didn't feel right to be laughing about it.

"Hey, I'm just messing with you, Wayne," he said, patting me on the back.

I faked a smile. How could he know what it felt like to be a plane-crash survivor? Not very many people did. We were a small but tight club.

Then I waited to see if anyone would talk to me or point at my face. But the lights were low and the music was turned up high and everyone was in a party mood.

"Go say hi to Carrot and Stephanie, why don't ya?" Dad said.

Stephanie was my Dad's new wife. His new kid was named Garrett, but everyone called him Carrot. I checked my watch. Why was Carrot still awake? When

I'd come to my dad's house at night before, Carrot was always in bed.

I wrote a note: *Carrot's awake?*

"Why not! It's New Year's Eve," Dad said.

Dad walked with me to Carrot's room, his hand still around my shoulders. Only now, it didn't feel friendly. It felt like a shove. He opened Carrot's door. Carrot was on the floor on top of a rug that had little streets printed on it. He was running his cars up and down the streets.

"Hey, hon, look who's finally here," Dad said.

"Hi, Wayne," Stephanie said. "Did you get something to eat?"

I needed to write all-purpose notes about my limited ability to eat. I would do that later. For now, I wrote: *Thanks.*

Carrot looked up at me, pointed at my head, and shouted for his mother. "Mama!" He ran and hid behind Stephanie.

"It's okay. It's just Wayne. He's here to play with you," Stephanie said.

"No, Mama!"

"Don't be such a crybaby, Carrot," Dad said. "It's fine." My dad left the room and went back to the party.

Carrot looked at me and squinted. He was still a little scared of my new face. Who could blame him?

I waved to him.

"Your face is messed up," Carrot said. "What happened?"

So my dad hadn't told him about the accident? Figured.

I scanned the room for a toy airplane. There had to be one there. Carrot's room was a virtual toy store. Sure enough, I found a blue-and-white model prop plane, flew it, and let it fall onto the carpet.

"Okay," he said. "This is my favorite car." He picked up a red Matchbox race car.

After a while, I heard fireworks go off. Carrot looked scared. A loud *BOOM*. And then *POP, POP, POP*. Carrot's eyes were wide. He looked at Stephanie with a question on his face. *Should I cry or not?*

"Oh, what is he doing now?" Stephanie got off the floor and left the room. Carrot and I followed her.

In the living room, Dad was sitting on the old futon, setting off tiny fireworks across the coffee table. Yep. In the living room, across the coffee table. His friends were laughing and slapping him on the back. The next one to go off had a rapid-fire bang. It shot up three or four times and blackened the ceiling.

I coughed on the smoke and went dizzy. The ground fell out from underneath me. My chest hurt.

Don't panic.

"You look green, Wayne," Dad said. "Hey, here, set this off."

He forced one into my hand. I didn't know what to do with it, so I shook my head.

"Come on and have some fun, Wayne!" He set off a sparkler, and it might have been pretty except that the smell of it choked me. I stumbled back onto the futon.

I couldn't breathe. My throat tightened. I coughed again. I suddenly thought, *I shouldn't be here*. Nobody *should be here*. I grabbed Carrot and lit out through the front door. The smell of burning chemicals followed me. I gulped down the fresh outside air and bolted down the block. When I got to the streetlamp, I realized I still had Carrot in my arms.

What am I doing?

Carrot had that look on his face like he might cry any second.

I walked back down the street with Carrot. I patted him on the back.

It's okay, Carrot.

Man, I wanted to talk to him, to say everything was okay and not to be scared. His face was red. I knew he was probably as confused as I was.

Down the street, another neighbor set off a load of fireworks. The stench of sulfur and smoke hung in the air.

They went off again and again. It sounded like gunfire. So I carried Carrot to my dad's front yard. There was Stephanie, hand on her hip, giving me a funny look.

"What are you doing, Wayne?" she asked. "That's not very responsible, you know?"

She took Carrot from me and went back inside. I stood there like a stump. Like a stupid, hollowed-out block of wood.

I couldn't go back inside. Loud pops and crackles were still going off. The music seemed to be louder. Someone popped a balloon. My heart raced. The earth felt like it was moving too fast underneath my feet. I thought I might throw up. And there it was. The exact same panic I had that day he did what he did back when I was eight.

I raced away from the neighborhood. I didn't plan to. I ran, and once I was moving, I couldn't stop. The sounds and the smoke and the dizzy feeling in my head forced me to the ground a couple of times. I tripped, scuffing my palms on the pavement. I guessed at where I was going. Was it two left turns out of his subdivision? Is that where it intersected with Crossland Road, one of the main streets between my house and Dad's? My phone was in my pocket. I could text Mom. Grandpa would have to come get me. There would be that look in his eyes. That *I told you so* look.

I ran faster.

My jacket was back at my dad's house. The cold night air chilled me to the bone. I tried to warm up by stepping up my pace. Then, relief! I finally sighted Crossland Road. There were plenty of cars racing down the road, people shouting *Happy New Year!* or *Woo-woo!* It was after midnight. The year had turned. Everyone in the world was happy. Everyone.

The inside of my body began to warm up. My ankle was tender and sore, but I wasn't going back. No way. Not inside that house where he was trying to catch everything on fire. Even I knew that.

I kept running, streetlight to streetlight. Then the water tower. The water tower that watched over Cedar Drive with its steady red light. Nerd alert: A guy has never been so happy to see a water tower.

True story.

It was my compass. And it made me swallow the panic.

The sky had turned dark blue and clear, or maybe it had been that way all along and I just couldn't see it through the smoke or didn't notice it because I was dizzy. But now that I knew the way home, I focused on it. I made out the Big Dipper. I saw two planes crossing over, too. Full of passengers celebrating New Year's Eve in the sky. People looking across the aisle, wishing a stranger a happy new year. It all made me think of 14A. So I quit thinking about it.

I turned onto Dogwood Street and then made a left onto Cedar Drive, where it was pretty quiet. I could hear my own breathing. Could hear my feet hit the pavement at a steady pace. I ran right in the middle of the road because, why not? Who would know?

I found the key to our house in the secret place Mom hides it. But I saw the blue light from the TV, which meant Grandpa was still up. It was too cold to wait it out, so I put the key in the lock.

The house was just the way I like a house—with no stupid people shooting off explosives inside it. Thankfully, Grandpa was in the big chair, snoring.

I ran to my room, closed the door quietly, and fell back onto my bed. I took deep, painful breaths through my raggedy throat. I tried to get my heart to slow down. Get my head on straight. Let my face thaw out and stop stinging. Make my ankle stop throbbing. It was like all my aches and injuries had been running five feet behind me and had suddenly caught up. I was in bad shape. I couldn't risk going to the kitchen for ice.

Why couldn't you just call Grandpa to pick you up, you dummy? Your ankle wouldn't hurt. Your throat wouldn't be on fire. Why didn't you just call?

But I knew why. I didn't call because we'd both have to admit that my dad could be a jerk. And yeah, he had done a really jerky thing tonight. But it's one thing to call your own parent a jerk. You don't want anyone else to do it. You'd rather feel sore all over and hope someone whose name rhymes with mad worries about how you got home.

True story.

CHAPTER 11

I woke up the next morning to the sound of my phone buzzing. Maybe it was the Flee wondering where I was.

Hola, Señor Kovok. Happy New Year.
Hola, Señorita Sandy. Cómo estás?
Muy bien! Look on your porch!

Nope. No messages from my dad.

Sandy had sent a big basket of muffins to our house, along with a Happy New Year card. Even though muffin consumption was going to be far beyond my abilities for a while, I loved that Sandy had thought of me. So I decided I would find a way to make the muffins useful. I put the basket on our kitchen counter and went out into the backyard with a single muffin. Blueberry.

I lay down on the hard, cold New Year's grass and used the muffin as a head support. It failed. It failed epically, but I didn't care.

I lay there and scouted for planes flying overhead. I'd fallen asleep the night before thinking about all the 14As who crossed my airspace every single day. All those strangers above the earth. All of them, like me and Mom, who just wanted to get home safe.

It was a fast-moving sky filled with thin clouds. I waited and watched for a plane to fly over. I put my hand up to the sky and positioned it underneath the belly of the first plane I spotted and held it there. I carried it for the time it took to cross my personal airspace. Twenty-eight seconds.

Be safe, plane.

Do you know what Orville Wright once said about the physics of flight? He said that "the airplane stays up because it doesn't have time to fall."

Because it doesn't have time to fall. Is that a good reason to fly? A way to make a person feel safe? Maybe.

Do you know that more people die each year from shaking a vending machine than from shark attacks?

True story.

People are afraid of sharks. But have you ever heard of

a vending machine phobia? Not me. Maybe there should be a show called *Deadliest Snacks*.

Someone with a loud, Tim LeMoot, the Texas Boot, ALL-CAPS voice could shout, *YOUR NEXT CANDY BAR COULD BE YOUR LAST!*

Some people are afraid to fly, too, but it doesn't stop thousands of people from traveling.

Every day in the United States, more than twenty-seven thousand commercial flights take off.

I looked it up.

That means that thousands of people were floating seven miles above the earth right as I was lying down, all relying on Orville Wright's theory that planes don't have time to fall.

All those planes.

And maybe even a hidden crocodile. There was a good chance that at least one out of six thousand flights carried a dork who'd smuggled a live animal on board.

I carried a second plane. Twenty-nine seconds.

I pictured the woman in 14A. Smiling, showing me her red-and-green quilted tree skirt. I still wished I'd talked to her on our flight.

So I made up other people inside the fuselage. Families. A woman reading a paperback. A guy playing a video game. Oh, and there's a flight attendant handing out snacks, and she looks just like my math teacher, Mrs. Wiggington. Mrs. W always smiled as she handed out math worksheets.

Be safe, Mrs. W.

I closed my eyes. The clouds had thinned out. Sun hit my backyard. My face was warm. Maybe today would be a good day, I thought. Maybe it would be the day Liz Delaney found the flag. And the empty space on the wall could be filled. Everything put in place. I let my mind go there, float. Mom with a smile, less one eyebrow. Grandpa informing me that I'd been useful because I'd thought to contact Ms. Delaney.

My mind unfolded. Relaxed. Went off on a trip to a warm place where there were no fireworks or sore ankles.

It was a great fantasy.

I would have let my mind stay gone all day.

But a long, tall, square-shouldered, aviator-sunglasses-wearing shadow eclipsed the sun. I looked up and squinted.

"Wayne, have you parted company with your senses? You realize you are lying on your dog's latrine."

I rolled over, stood up, and brushed dry grass from my jeans. Grandpa was consuming one of *my* muffins. My one gift from the girl of my dreams.

"I didn't hear your father's car drive up last night," he said, hands on his hips.

I shrugged. *You can't hear what's not there.*

"Your mother needs your help washing her hair. Can you do it?"

I helped Mom wash her hair in the kitchen sink.

"Are you excited about going to the new school next week?"

I nodded yes. I'd never lied to Mom with a gesture before.

"Nice of Sandy to send those muffins," Mom said. She seemed better than the previous day. Maybe she thought the new year was going to be, well, new.

"Want to watch a movie later?"

Do I get to pick?

"Sure," she said. No sad smile. "Oh, your dad called and said he was going to drop off your jacket. Guess you left it there?"

I shrugged.

"Wayne? Honey, do you ever want to talk to anyone about the crash? A counselor? If you do, let me know. We could do it together, okay?" She touched my face.

No, even if I could actually talk, I didn't want to talk to a counselor. I just needed the flag to be found, Grandpa to move back to his house, my face and neck to heal, my dad to stop messing with me, and Mom to keep smiling and make spaghetti every Tuesday. That was all. I no longer even cared if we ever got a dishwasher. I didn't mind washing dishes.

I knew what I wanted. So what was there to talk about?

I smiled at her because I knew that was what *she* wanted, and then I went out the front door.

My skateboard was leaning against the brick. I flung it on the sidewalk and took off. I wasn't going to be home when the Flee showed up. No way.

I skateboarded way past our block. Past Elm and Dogwood and Oak Streets. Deep into the new neighborhood called the Estates. It was set right against our forest of streets. For me, the best thing about the Estates wasn't the new houses. It was the new streets. Smooth, even, and acorn-free. Perfect for skateboarding. I skated all the way to the park, where eighty-year-old trees shaded the playground equipment in summertime. I climbed up into the plastic spaceship that had been bright red when we moved there but was now faded to pale pink. I'd only intended to sit there with my thoughts for a short time and look at planes and think about what I might text to Sandy. But a mom and her two kids came to the park. They played on the swings and laughed. I didn't want to scare them with my face the way I'd scared Carrot. And since I had no voice to explain to the mother that I wasn't a murdery stalker, I stayed up in that spaceship until dark.

DATA

Flight 56 debris found 15 miles east of crash site.

Question: How large is total debris field?

Tasks: Obtain map of East Texas. Monitor collection of all debris.

CHAPTER 12

My whole life, I'd been pretty good at avoiding mirrors. But since I became a plane-crash survivor, I learned that people were like mirrors. And they were harder to avoid.

I'd covered the bathroom mirror with a towel. Grandpa took it down. I covered it with six sheets of paper. He crumpled those up.

"What's the meaning of this?" he asked.

I pointed to my face. I thought my meaning was obvious.

"Don't be so dramatic. So you have some cuts. Big deal," he said.

My stitches were those self-absorbing ones. They had completely disappeared the week before. You would think this was an improvement in how I looked, but no, it wasn't. Now I had a pink L-shaped scar down my face.

The doctor told Mom I had to wear these bright white butterfly-shaped bandages across the scar to keep from tearing the skin. There were three of them on my face, from my eyebrow to my jawline. And the bruises on my chin and cheek? They had morphed from purple into a yellow-green color.

So my beat-up look was just as obvious as it had been the day the plane crashed. My face was changing colors like a mood ring. And maybe Grandpa didn't think it was a big deal because he and I still hadn't looked at each other directly since that awful day in the kitchen when I'd seen him, well, you know. The thing with the waterworks.

So I put my towel back over the bathroom mirror.

Mom said my changing face was a good sign. I was healing.

A good sign?

No way.

Not a good look for a guy about to attend the West Academy for the very first time.

That morning, it was cold. I could see my breath against the window as I watched my old school bus cruise past my house. I stood at the window like a dog waiting for its owner to come back home.

Pathetic.

Maybe I didn't want to ride the bus. Maybe I didn't

want to run like a maniac down the sidewalk. I told myself I was glad I wouldn't have to see mustard balls hurled my way. Or unpredictable seventh graders calling me Wayne-a-Pedia. Or annoy Carl, the bus driver.

Because plane-crash bonus number twenty-seven: I had a new Carl now. Grandpa. Grandpa was going to drive me to and from school. And it was going to drive me crazy.

We got into his old truck. His "everyday car," as he called it. No way I'd get to ride in the Car.

"Don't leave any of your pencils behind," Grandpa said.

I gave him a look. *What?*

"You used to do that all the time when you were little," he said. "Leave your things all over the place."

I would not comment on all the Grandpa stuff lined up on *my* bathroom counter. I would not.

"Who ironed those pants?" Grandpa asked. "They need an exact crease."

I looked at my pants. They looked fine to me.

"I'll teach you the correct way later."

So this was how my new ride to school would be. Another opportunity to disappoint Grandpa. Do more things wrong. Great.

Maybe I could figure out how far away the school was from our house. I could walk. I'd probably do that wrong, too.

The West Academy looked less like an academy and more like a doctor's office. A one-level brick-and-glass building. We all wore the same uniform: white shirt and navy pants. From the neck down, I could pretty much pass for every other kid there.

And it wasn't really within walking distance from Cedar Drive. Unless I wanted to start walking to school before the sun came up.

Double great.

I walked into my first class. No one noticed me. They were all so busy being talented or special that I barely registered a nod from the guy in front of me.

I walked into my second class. Only one guy spoke to me. "Hey, what happened to your face?"

I pulled out a note card. I'd pre-written several responses to speed up communication.

Studying the effects of zero gravity. Dangerous experiment.

"Oh, you're that airplane guy," he said. "They told us to expect you." He turned around and put his head into a book.

That was it. Everyone at West was white shirt, navy pants, head down, get the lesson done, and go be super talented. There wasn't even a cafeteria. So there was no need to worry about where to sit.

Where had this school been my whole life?

My yellow-green-bruised, pink-scarred face didn't cause kids to run screaming down the hallway or even render a head tilt.

I allowed myself to be happy. Hopeful, even.

I felt like I fit in. I mean, it was great. A fresh start.

Almost.

At the West Academy, I had to attend for only half a day. I got to leave at noon. At the end of that first day, I attempted a smile at a group of pretty girls in ponytails. I later found out they were a trio of champion gymnasts.

They recoiled with the kind of agility you'd expect from pretty gymnasts: in perfect head-tilt, mouth-open unison.

True story.

After school, Grandpa picked me up.

"Next stop, voice doctor," Grandpa announced. Mom had found "the perfect voice specialist" for me. His name was Dr. Pajaczkowski, and he made me spend an hour making small sounds and breathing deeply. It hurt to practice, but that was what I was supposed to do if I ever wanted to have a normal voice. Or eat my favorite foods.

Grandpa and I sat in Dr. Pajaczkowski's waiting room. There was a sliding glass window behind which an older lady in a brown sweater sat. Her sweater reminded me of 14A.

While I waited, Grandpa read magazines and I learned that the kid across from me was named Denny Rosenblatt. Not because I had psychic powers but because Brown-Sweatered Receptionist called out, "Denny Rosenblatt."

Denny Rosenblatt and mother of Denny Rosenblatt went behind the door. Mother of Denny Rosenblatt must have been very happy to be there because she was smiling the whole time. Denny Rosenblatt looked happy, too, which was nice because he reminded me of those kids who got picked on for no good reason. You know that kid with curly hair who is kind of small for his age, carries a band instrument, and has a hard time finding a place to sit on the bus? That was Denny.

But Denny also looked like that kid who would let *me* sit next to him on the bus. Let's face it. I was always looking for that kind of kid. We'd probably both get picked on, but if we sat together, who would care?

Ten minutes later Brown-Sweatered Receptionist called, "Wayne Kovok."

"Ten-hut, Kovok," Grandpa said. "Don't keep people waiting!"

Did you know that the military shout *ten-hut* is an abbreviation of the word *attention*? It's thought that shouting *Attention!* doesn't get troop attention. The phrase *ten-hut* does. Guess who has told me that fact since I was four years old? Guess who thinks I'm like my dad, who always keeps people waiting? I'll tell you who. Someone with a name that rhymes with *Sand Paw*!

I grunted at Grandpa.

I went behind the door and sat in a white room with a white linoleum table and waited for Dr. Pajaczkowski. On the walls of the exam room, there were all kinds of pictures of the vocal anatomy. Tongues. Vocal cords. Tonsils. The whole enchilada of the human mouth. It looked fascinating. It also looked pink and gross.

"How're we doing today, Wayne? Feeling better?" Dr. Pajaczkowski said. He walked into the room with a file and a smile.

I hummed at him.

"Open wide," Dr. Pajaczkowski said.

We did a series of exercises that involved me "making good use of airway management."

How long until I can talk? I wrote to him.

"When you can pronounce my name, I will pronounce you healed!" Dr. Pajaczkowski said. "But for what you've experienced, you're doing well, Wayne."

If the sound of heavy breathing and trying to whisper the sound *e* is good, I guess I was doing well. My voice sounded ridiculous. Like a zombie with a sinus infection.

"You're really doing great, Wayne," Dr. P said. "I want

you to remember that more than sixty percent of communication is nonverbal. You can still be heard."

You can still be heard if someone is looking at you. But what if he doesn't look at you until he wants you to go and be useful in another room? Or what if he doesn't even notice that you've run away from his New Year's Eve party? You can't be heard then, Dr. P.

Through the office walls, I heard someone singing. And I guess I used some of my nonverbal communication with my right eyebrow, because Dr. P said, "Oh, you hear that? That's the sound of progress!"

When I came out into the hall, I saw the face of progress. Denny Rosenblatt stood there singing. When he saw me, he instantly stopped and looked at me the way everyone did now, only with a little extra...something. With a curious head tilt, a scrunched-up nose, and a chin rub. His nonverbal communication was loud.

"Secret ninja fight?" he asked in a whispery voice.

I flashed him my all-purpose note card about my zero-gravity experiment.

"I'd go with the secret-ninja story," he whispered, and then smiled.

Grandpa and I rode the elevator back to the ground level with the Rosenblatts. I hated that elevator. Solid mirrors from ceiling to floor. I studied my shoes and listened as Denny sang about cheeseburgers to the tune of the "Happy Birthday" song.

"I want a cheeseburger, please. I want a cheeseburger, please. I want a *cheese*burger, pul-EEZE. I want a cheeseburrrgerrrrr. Pleeeeeease!"

"Denny, try to talk," said the still-smiling mother of Denny Rosenblatt. "It's the strangest thing. Denny can sing perfectly, but he stammers a little when he talks."

"I s-s-stutter a lot," Denny said. And then he broke out in song, "It's all about air management!"

Denny Rosenblatt had a good singing voice. There was no trace of stuttering when Denny Rosenblatt sang. Dr. P was right. Denny was the voice of progress.

I wondered if Denny could pronounce Dr. P's name in song.

Denny tried to speak to his mother, but the word *want* seemed stuck on the way out of his mouth. He caught me staring at him, and then he pointed to my face and sang, "What happened in your experiment exactly? What happened with zero gravity?"

All I could do was shrug and grunt while we waited for the elevator door to open.

"Kid's messed up," Grandpa said.

Mrs. Rosenblatt stepped out of the elevator with Denny, then pulled her son close like she was protecting him. From me. From Grandpa. I realized she thought Grandpa had called Denny messed up. If you think we had a very uncomfortable walk to the parking lot, you would be correct.

"A cheeseburger sounds good," Grandpa said. "You like those shakes at Sonic."

Man, he was reading my thoughts again in his weird Grandpa way. Yes, a cheeseburger did sound good and I *did* like those shakes at Sonic. But I really didn't want to hang out with Grandpa. Maybe that sounds mean, but drinking a shake was probably on the long list of things I did that annoyed him. I didn't have a choice, though.

Grandpa drove to Sonic and ordered a vanilla shake for me and a cheeseburger for himself. Man, the smell of the juicy cheeseburger was pure torture. I had to keep myself from drooling. Then we went to the pet store to buy food for Hank Williams. Hank Williams ate more solid food than I did.

If you want to know, I hated that fact. My clothes were loose. My stomach growled all the time. Last week, I had a dream about chasing a life-sized doughnut.

True story.

And then, did you know I was blamed for Grandpa eating a cheeseburger? I couldn't even drive, yet I was still responsible for the two-patty, double-cheese, heavy pickle lunch that Grandpa heaved into the toilet when we got home.

Mom scowled at me and said, "How could you let him eat a cheeseburger?" Like I could stop him from doing anything. I wrote back to her on my notepad: Why can't he eat a burger?

"How was school?" Mom asked. "School was good?"

I shoved the paper in front of her again. She didn't respond, so I wrote: What's wrong with him?

This made her face change. Her eyes turned down.

I knew that look. The worried face. The face that was worried about Grandpa, who was sad about Uncle Reed, which led to thoughts about the crash and finally a thought about the missing flag. Do you know what? I hoped that when we found the flag, it would be one less reason for Mom to be sad. One less.

"Well, I think he might be coming down with a cold. And also, he got a message today about Reed and..." She didn't finish. She rubbed her finger over one of the frames on the Wall of Honor.

You know that saying "There's an elephant in the room," which means there's a subject no one wants to talk about?

Yeah, I'd looked up the phrase a few years back when a teacher tossed it out in class and it made me curious.

Lately, any mention of Uncle Reed was the ultimate elephant-in-the-room kind of topic. Like the largest elephant to ever walk the planet, which, if you want to know, was an African elephant weighing thirteen and a half tons. My sixth-grade social studies teacher said that was equal to 165 grown men.

True story.

For a minute, I imagined 165 people inside our house on Cedar Drive. No way they would all fit.

So both of us stood in the hallway and listened to Grandpa get sick. This is not what a person who is retching wants you to do.

Grandpa came out, said, "At ease," and headed for his room.

Mom reached to touch my face in the mom way again.

"Should I change your bandages?" she asked.

And I backed up and got my face away from her hand and ran my head right into the Wall of Honor. My great-grandfather, RB Dalton, fell off the wall. I caught the frame before it bounced.

Mom took me by the shoulder and ushered me to the kitchen, and we both drank strawberry smoothies. That was when I saw the basket. Another big basket of muffins on the counter. Apple cinnamon.

More food I couldn't eat.

"Yeah. Those. Those were on the porch. From Sandy's mother," Mom said. "I talked to her. Sandy wants to know if she can come over. She also suggested that you could come to one of Beatty's school games."

I shook my head. The mirrored reflection I feared most was in Sandy Showalter's blue eyes.

"Are you going to call her?"

And do what, Mom? Breathe into the phone?

"Well, Grandpa could drive you to the game. Or, hey, your dad."

Never going to happen.

"Well, send her a note or something and thank her. Want me to tell you something about girls?"

Nope.

Mom said, "The thing about girls is that if you don't keep in touch, they will think you don't like them. So decide how much this is worth to you. It might feel good to go and do something normal."

I gave Mom a thumbs-up. *Normal. Got it. Wayne Kovok is nothing if not normal.*

"Why don't you take Mr. Darcy for a walk?" she asked.

I grabbed Mr. Darcy's leash and shook it, which always gets him up and running. He ran into the kitchen, and I latched the leash onto his collar.

The door clicked closed right as Mom said she loved me.

121

Did you know that the French word for *bad* is *mal*? So half of *normal* is bad.

The Latin origin of this word, *normalis*, is translated as "made from a carpenter's square." So if something is made by a carpenter, and there are different carpenters in the world, then not every square is going to be *normalis*. That is the variable in the science experiment of life. If I had a voice, I would shout, *Not everything is normal!*

New topic.

Did you know that pilots sometimes use water towers to aid in navigation? Most small towns paint the town name on the tower, and if a pilot lacks a GPS system, he can get his bearings by reading the towers. One town in South Carolina painted its tower to look like a giant peach. In my town, we are known for giant shopping malls, bad drivers, and intense summer heat. Maybe our tower should have flames and an advertisement for women's jewelry.

Here's a *Jeopardy!* question: This seventh-grade dork thinks too much about water towers.

Answer: Who is Wayne Kovok?

I wondered if I could put a towel over my face *and* my thoughts. I mean, who thinks of these things?

I lay down on the sidewalk to clear my head. Even though the concrete was freezing, it was *not* my dog's latrine, thank you very much! It was outside where I hoped there was zero chance I would be doing something in violation of the correct Grandpa code. I waited for a plane. Good old Mr. Darcy snuggled against me. I ferried six planes over Cedar Drive. They all made it. They all survived to live another day. Just like me.

DATA

Non-aircraft Flight 56 debris found in East Texas since the crash:

- *Suitcases*

- *A Bible*

- *A gold wedding ring, ripped in half*

- *A travel guide:* What to Do in Dallas?

- *A charred teddy bear*

- *A Minnie Mouse lunch box*

- *Assorted clothing and shoes found hung in nearby pine trees*

CHAPTER 13

Two days later, Grandpa picked me up late from the West Academy. So late, in fact, that I'd sat on the outside steps and watched three planes, a thick bank of clouds, and the trio of gymnasts go past me. The gymnasts all waved to me in perfect unison. Word had definitely gotten around that I'd survived a plane crash. In second-period science, the teacher, Mr. Clark, said, "Wayne is pretty special. The odds of surviving a plane crash are pretty low."

Everyone in class had turned to look at me.

Special Wayne.

I really needed a fact shield at that moment. I could have blurted out, *Did you know your lifetime odds of dying in an airplane crash are about one in eight thousand? Did you know your lifetime odds of dying in a car crash are about one in one hundred?*

So please turn around and focus on Mr. Clark instead of me.

I registered their looks as equal parts pity and curiosity.

I was trying not to care what strangers thought of my look. Trying and failing.

"I'm late," Grandpa announced as I got into his truck, as if it weren't obvious.

I thought being on time was a virtue! I guess Daltons can be late, too. Ha!

"Your mother's at an appointment, so I'll drop you at home before I head to the store. Unless you want to go to the store?"

I shook my head.

"Maybe you want to play poker later? Your mother thinks I should teach you," he said.

Why?

"So you'll know how to play," he said.

Okay.

Great. Another opportunity to feel dumb around Grandpa. I made a mental note to talk about this with Mom. She was still on a quest for me to learn "man things."

Once I was in the house, I began composing what I thought had the potential for a poetic text to Sandy. I was attempting to take some of Mom's advice.

Dearest Sandy,

Roses are red. The sky is blue. The muffins were yummy. How is school?

Okay, my attempt wasn't Shakespearean. But I mean, Shakespeare's first drafts probably weren't perfect, right?

I stared out the window at the tree and sky in our front yard. I could rhyme *tree* with *Sandy*. Or even with *the Flee.*

I watched the Flee park his car in front of our house. I tried to remember if I'd gotten a text from him. Nope. If he was supposed to come over. Nope. Maybe this was more of Mom's idea. Either way, I was going to pretend I wasn't home.

He strolled up the walk, his hands stuffed into his pockets, his work shirt with his name and employer stitched on a badge: DOUG and LPS PLUMBING in white lettering. He didn't have my jacket with him.

He knocked on the door.

I ignored it.

"Hi, Wayne, open up. I know you're in there. I saw your grandfather drop you off."

Knock. Knock. Knock.

I opened the door.

I scribbled a note, tore off the paper, and shoved it out

126

the door. The Flee read it and frowned. "What do I want? Is that any way to talk to your father?"

It seemed right to me.

"So, listen, can you come over to the house? Stephanie's dad is a lawyer, and he's there right now. He'd like to ask you some questions about the airline case," he said, pushing his way farther into the house.

What's our case?

"Well, that's the thing. We don't know if you have a larger case. So he'd like to get a statement from you. See what your position is."

I wrote: I don't know.

But I did know. Mom had told me we weren't joining any lawsuit. She'd settled with the airline.

We got out with our lives. The airline is paying all our bills and giving us a settlement right now if we don't sue. There'll be enough to replace the broken dishwasher, she'd said, happy. She was ready to put all this behind her, and a friend had told her the lawsuit might drag on. I thought that was smart and told her so. Then I told her I'd rather have a new computer than a dishwasher.

What about both? she'd said. *I just found out about this iPad app that will talk for you. Wouldn't that be cool?*

I thought it might be cool. Or maybe I'd sound like a digital nerd. Like a seventh-grade Stephen Hawking.

So I wasn't going to say anything to my dad. Mom told me not to talk to the Flee about it.

"Hey, get me a glass of water, would you? Your mom won't be back for a while."

Wait, what? How did he know Mom was gone?

I got him a glass of water. Before you knew it, we were standing in the kitchen and the Flee was moving Mom's blue glass birds around on the counter.

"Don't know why she liked these stupid birds," he said. *Because they were her mother's birds.*

Then he pawed around at the Sandy Showalter basket of muffins like they belonged to him. My neck started to burn hot with aggravation. If the Flee said or did one more thing, I might go up in flames.

"Look at those tennis shoes," the Flee said. "What are those, anyway?"

He had to do it. One more thing.

I looked down at my feet. That's where the flames would come from. From my used shoes. Pity shoes. *Duuuude, your face* shoes, so why can't you just get out of my kitchen now?

"How about we go get you some new ones? Write your mom a note on that silly little pad around your neck." He took another drink of water.

I lied on a note. Can't go. Dr. appointment.

"Well, I'll take you."

Talk to Mom.

" 'Talk to Mom'? Don't be such a mama's boy, Wayne. Your mom doesn't know all the questions to ask."

Please leave.

He tossed my note onto the linoleum but kept eating a muffin. Half of it crumbled to the floor.

"Look, it's no big deal," he said as he lazily pushed the dropped pieces of muffin underneath the cabinet with his foot. As if that took care of the problem. "I just want you to explain to the lawyer the accident details, like whether your mom was injured because she unbuckled her seat belt trying to get that silly flag. You didn't unbuckle yours, right?"

No.

I was certain that my entire face had gone tomato red.

Mom had to unbuckle on the plane. I let go of the flag. Every time I pictured the flag escaping the plane, my chest felt heavy. I wanted to hide from that fact, but there was no place to go. The flag just had to be found. Period. The airline couldn't replace that.

He poked his head in our refrigerator and pulled out the milk. He shook the carton, which was almost empty. "She still doesn't know how to keep house. Where are the sodas?"

My neck got hotter and I got a sick feeling in my stomach. I didn't want new shoes from him. I'd always look down at them and remember him saying mean things about Mom. I'd rather look at stupid Goodwill shoes.

I wrote him a note: Can't go.

"Wayne, don't be such a pain. Let's get some shoes and a bite to eat."

I shook my head again.

"Come on!" He slapped his hand on the countertop. I froze. For a minute, I thought maybe I should go with him and not make anything worse. He took a deep sigh and drummed his fingers on the countertop. Mom's blue glass birds were awfully close to his hands.

He took me by the sleeve of my hoodie and pushed me toward the front door. Now that we were clear of the kitchen, of the birds, I jerked my arm out of his grip. I shook my head *no*, and I wrote it on my notepad with several exclamation points following just so that he could hear my tone. I saw the flash in his eyes. I knew it was coming.

"Now, you stop it!" The Flee clipped the left side of my head with his hand. Normally, I wouldn't have felt anything but a thump. But now the left side of my face felt everything. I didn't even sleep on my left side anymore.

So my skin burned.

And stung.

It hurt like a million tiny darts hitting my forehead. I held my breath. I fought to keep the tears away. I wouldn't show the pain. I would not.

"Kovok!" Grandpa said, surprising us both.

Grandpa wasn't just a former army drill sergeant. He had been chosen to *teach* drill sergeant school. When he turned on that voice, it was full of thunder. More than once in my life, it had scared me senseless. But at that moment, his voice wasn't directed at me. I felt a tiny bit of relief. No, actually I felt a big wave of relief. The Flee wouldn't dare be a Grade A jerk in front of Grandpa.

"Take it easy, old man," the Flee said.

Then again . . .

"Coming into my house and touching my family! Exactly who do you think you are?"

Grandpa stared down the Flee with the intensity of a laser beam. I'm not joking. And the Flee backed into the front door, then shook a little. "I'm his father. I can come over here anytime I want."

"You seem a little confused on the facts," Grandpa said. "Wayne, I feel like getting a cheeseburger. Go wait in the Car while I straighten out Mr. Kovok on the facts."

I scribbled on my notepad. THE car?

"Affirmative."

I took a few slow steps backward toward the garage. Because who wanted to stop watching this showdown?

The Flee shifted his weight from side to side. Nervous.

Grandpa crossed his arms and kept his eyes leveled at the Flee. Confident.

Dr. P was right about nonverbal communication. Just looking at the Flee versus Grandpa, you knew who would win on the battlefield. Who would turn and run, and who would stay and fight. Lazy Kovoks on one side. Hero Daltons on the other.

What did that make me?

For a split second, I turned my head away. I didn't like what I was seeing. Because maybe I was seeing the Flee the way Grandpa saw him. As a darn Kovok.

I felt dazed and even more sick to my stomach.

"Wayne, you don't have to do what he says," the Flee said, locking eyes with me. "You can come with me." He grinned, and it made him look stupid. Like a stupid Kovok.

Grandpa turned and gave me the slightest nod.

My chest tightened and my head throbbed. There was a tug-of-war going on there in the entryway of my house, and I was the rope. The rope never wins. It just gets pulled.

I broke out of my daze and headed toward the garage. Maybe Grandpa saw a darn Kovok junior when I was around.

I stood in front of the Car, feeling dizzy. I told my brain to go someplace better.

I closed my eyes and remembered a Bear Ball hitting me in the chest, knocking the air out of me. Yes, that is the stupid memory my brain selected for me. Bear Ball. Bear Ball is a game they play at Beatty Middle School. Two captains are chosen, and then they choose their teams. The PE coaches think they're giving us a treat when they say, *You can go play Bear Ball now.*

It is not a treat.

Last time, I was the second-to-last to be picked. The last one picked was a small girl. We were the leftovers.

The only time a leftover is good is when it's pizza.

Trey Harris picked me. "That's just Kovok." For everyone else, he'd introduced the person by his or her talent. Good at passing the ball. Fast on the court. But me? I was just Kovok. Picked by default. And when that happens, you have to try to show some skills or risk ultimate humiliation. You have to prove they were right to pick you. Instead, you end up proving they were right to pick you last.

Because when you are nervous and annoyed, you

suck. And you wish that the gym floor would open up into a black hole. Because then you'd be known as that guy who disappeared into the floor instead of "just Kovok."

You see how it is inside my head now that my mouth can't speak and all these thoughts have no place to go? Do you see?

CHAPTER 14

I stood in the garage, wishing a black hole would open up underneath me.

Grandpa was just taking me to Sonic and letting me ride in the Car by default.

I'd never ridden in the Car. The Mustang. The red Ford convertible so shiny you could check your teeth in it. The *do not touch this under penalty of death* vehicle.

So when Grandpa came out into the garage an eternity after he'd put the Flee in a corner, I was still staring at it like the forbidden, expensive piece of artwork it was.

"You waiting for an engraved invitation?" he asked. And he looked me straight in the eye. He hadn't done that since that awkward day in the kitchen.

He eased himself into the driver's seat and then put

the key in the ignition. I buckled my seat belt and remembered to breathe.

"The thing you have to remember with old cars is that they don't just start up cold as soon as you turn the key. You have to pump the gas twice and then hold down the pedal."

He pumped the gas twice and got it started, and we drove at Grandpa speed out of the neighborhood. Do you know I can skateboard faster than he can drive?

True story.

I didn't mind. Even though it was chilly outside, Grandpa put the convertible top down. The sun poured into the car and warmed the leather seats. I got a good look at the inside of the Car. All original.

The seats were creamy-white leather with detailed ponies stitched into the backs. The dashboard was the same candy-apple red as the paint. Every time we stopped at a light, we got looks from the other drivers. Good looks, too. When we got to the last stoplight, I passed Grandpa a note: What happened?

"You don't worry about him, Wayne."

We parked outside the Sonic. Grandpa pushed the red button and ordered a cheeseburger and a root beer float. A carhop on roller skates delivered the food minutes later.

The icy drink felt good.

"Don't you even think about spilling anything on the Car."

I nodded.

"Don't tell your mother I'm eating a cheeseburger."

I nodded again.

"And don't tell your mother about the Flee. In fact, don't even think about the Flee."

My one usable eyebrow rose.

"Don't think about what happened today for another second. Darn Kovok, son of a gun. He was a loser from zero hour. Even your uncle Reed thought so."

I know.

Grandpa paused to take a bite of sweet root beer–flavored ice cream from my root beer float. "Reed. Now, that was a decent human being who would've made a great father. Solid. One of a kind, that one. Was carrying on the Dalton family name with honor. There's no one now, which is an injustice of colossal proportions. No one. Sad shame. Reed died with all my stories, all my advice, all the attributes that generations of Dalton men have carried since the time of the Revolutionary War. He was going to get this car next year. I find that ... unacceptable."

Maybe I hadn't just been hit square in the chest with a Bear Ball, but it felt like it. It wasn't just the wave of sadness about Reed I could hear in Grandpa's voice. It was how he'd turned and looked at me when he said the word *unacceptable*.

In the game of Bear Ball, all Daltons would get picked first. Kovoks last. We'd lose every time.

"Did I ever tell you about Henry Dalton, my great-grandfather, who fought in the Revolutionary War?" Grandpa asked.

Of course I'd heard all about Henry Dalton, who fought in the Revolutionary War, and all the other Daltons who were not like the Flee and me, about one thousand times. Well, twenty-four times to be precise. Three times a year on the major Grandpa holidays (Christmas, Thanksgiving, and Fourth of July) for the past eight years. In our family, holiday dinners were traditionally, but not intentionally, served cold. Grandpa's toasts about patriotism and freedom fighters made hot turkey and mashed potatoes a delicacy foreign to my taste buds.

True story.

So even if I'd had the full use of my voice, I wouldn't have responded. Grandpa was having a "memorial moment," as Mom called them. *Never interrupt when he does that.*

Somewhere around the time Henry Dalton had been gravely wounded in battle, taking his last breath on the "hard-won ground of a new nation," Grandpa had commandeered my root beer float to use as a prop illustrating incoming British soldiers.

"I'll get you new shoes, Wayne," Grandpa said. "Good running shoes, too. I know you're a good runner. You have the build for it, you know."

I let out a breath. I gave him a slight smile.

He rolled down the window of the Car and waved over the carhop, a boy who looked like he was barely in high school. I caught a glimpse of his name tag: TODD. Todd grabbed the first cup and then tripped and spilled root beer float down the door of the Car. THE. CAR!

"Oh, my bad, dude," Todd said. "Here are some napkins." He extended a handful of white Sonic napkins toward Grandpa.

Todd was digging his own grave with two shovels.

Grandpa opened his door slowly. He squared his shoulders and took two controlled steps toward Todd. He removed his aviator sunglasses. He inspected the Car. Then he tucked the napkins into Todd's shirt collar.

Todd looked like he was going to pee his pants.

Did you know that bladder control is connected to the brain? When the body is scared, it receives a rush of adrenaline, making you prepared to run or fight. Under stress, inhibitory signals from your brain's frontal lobe

139

can be overridden, and so you urinate in the presence of danger.

Todd was in the presence of danger.

And the expression on Todd's face indicated that his frontal lobe might have sent an evacuation signal.

"Soldier, you best go get your commander in chief!" Grandpa said quietly. Too quiet, if you asked me. Like calm-before-the-storm quiet.

I sat up higher to watch. I sort of liked seeing this version of Grandpa when it wasn't directed at me.

Sure enough, Grandpa and the Sonic manager began discussing how upholding customer-service policies was the first line of defense in a strong nation. I couldn't believe it. Todd stood there, shaking in his roller skates. I'll say this for him: At least he didn't skate away. A lot of guys would have.

Grandpa continued, "Buttercup, this may be challenging for your young mind to comprehend, but if you don't uphold the pillars of the American work ethic at a burger joint, you have not earned the right to wear *any* uniform. You have failed in your mission to bring dignity to a job that many would be privileged to have. There are no small jobs, only small people."

"Yes, sir."

Todd got on his knees and wiped away the vanilla ice-cream evidence with a special yellow cloth Grandpa had pulled from the trunk of the Car. Grandpa grimaced at Todd like he was doing it all wrong.

"You're doing it all wrong!" Grandpa shouted. He showed Todd how he'd wanted it done in the first place. "You know what Napoleon said, son?"

"Napoleon, sir?"

And I thought, *Here we go. The Napoleon lesson. This speech goes well with turkey and cranberry sauce.*

"Geography is destiny."

"Yes, sir."

"Your geography is the United States of America. Do you know what that makes you?"

Don't screw up now, Todd. This is actually a good lesson.

"No, sir," Todd said. "What does that make me?"

"Luckier than a great majority of the world who would love to trade places with you and live in a nation built on the backs of your forefathers and my forefathers and do a job—any job—the right way. Even at Sonic, son."

"Yes, sir."

"Will you be upholding the nation your forefathers built for you?"

"Yes, sir. Lots of upholding."

Todd was a quick learner.

All this excitement drew a small crowd. People got

served burgers with a side of Americana, and I guess they liked it better than fries. I couldn't figure out how he did it, but Grandpa made the link between a soldier's bravery and the ability to steady a Styrofoam cup seem realistic.

He made it sound as if dropping a plastic spoon or forgetting a straw would be letting our country down. I wished people who didn't pick up a crumbled muffin on my mom's kitchen floor could hear this lesson, too.

Volunteerism...

Nobility...

Service...

All of a sudden I caught a glimpse of how Grandpa must have looked to the men he trained in the army. He wasn't just a square-shouldered man with a big voice who told you what to do. He was a man who loved his country and made you want to love it, too.

Maybe I felt a little bit of pride.

I definitely felt a little bit of pride.

Okay, I felt a ton of pride.

Grandpa concluded his speech by talking about Reed Dalton, his brave son who served our country for fifteen years. Uncle Reed would have liked all the things Grandpa said about him. You know the way the hairs on the back of your neck stand up when you sing the national anthem sometimes? You feel connected to something larger. Well, that's how it was right there at Sonic, believe it or not. Reed was my uncle and I was connected to him. Really connected. I wanted Uncle Reed to be in the car with us. And Mom riding beside him. All of us, having shakes at Sonic together.

Somewhere in my strange brain, I caught a glimpse of the lost flag. Maybe it was all the patriotism, but I would have sworn I could see it flapping in the wind, waiting for me or Liz Delaney to find it and call it what it was. Miraculous. And me, handing it back to Mom. Grandpa smiling and nodding. Maybe today was the day it would be found.

The Sonic manager, who now had little imaginary American flags floating around his head, interrupted Grandpa's memorial moment and said, "So, where is Specialist Dalton now, sir? When he comes home, I'll give him free Cokes and burgers for life!"

The small crowd cheered.

Grandpa became silent as a rock.

All the animation in his body left him. All the confidence of his voice went away.

He quietly said, "My son rests heroically on the grounds of Arlington National Cemetery."

The thirteen-and-a-half-ton elephant in the room had jumped into the backseat of the Car and come with us to Sonic.

Stupid Todd. Stupid spilled drink.

Every good thing that had happened vanished in two seconds. Man, the day had had more highs and lows than a roller coaster.

Todd handed Grandpa the special yellow cloth, then opened the car door for him.

We didn't talk on the ride home. We kept the top down on the Car, and the cold wind rushed in. Two planes entered my sight path, one heading east and the other west. Two passengers in two separate 14A seats crisscrossing the sky. I supported them both until my arms could no longer stretch. I couldn't help it. Now when I saw planes, I had to do something.

Have a good trip.

Grandpa didn't seem to notice or care that his grand-son was holding the victory arms position. Maybe he did think I was messed up.

I don't have to tell you that the day ended with me in my same old, dingy Goodwill shoes. As soon as the Car came to a full stop in our garage, I ran to my room to retrieve my skateboard. And then I grabbed the scarf, the shemagh, that Uncle Reed had given me last Christmas.

I wrapped it around my neck. I thought it might conceal my scars if I got accidentally trapped in a pink playground spaceship again.

"Hey, you have an appointment later. Be back promptly," Grandpa said to me as I flew out the front door.

I headed up toward the perfect streets of the Estates. I chased after that free-floating feeling I'd had earlier in the day when the tug-of-war inside me had loosened. I even ditched my skateboard in someone's yard and ran and ran in my stupid Goodwill shoes until one of the soles came loose and all I could hear was *flop, flop, flop.*

It didn't matter. The feeling had outrun me, and I couldn't catch up. We forgot to play poker later. Well, *he* forgot. I didn't bring it up.

CHAPTER 15

If I was going to run, I was going to get better shoes. Really good shoes.

Did you know that track star Jesse Owens wore Adidas and he won four gold medals at the 1936 Olympics?

I wrote to Denny Rosenblatt: If Adidas were good enough for a champion, they are good enough for Wayne Kovok.

And Denny e-mailed back: Come to the mall. My mom works there.

The day before, Denny and I had sat in the waiting room of Dr. P's office and gotten to know each other.

As it turned out, Denny was really easy to be around.

I wrote to him: *You sing really well.*

So he sang-talked, "What really happened to your face?"

And I wrote: plane crash last December in East Texas.

Denny Rosenblatt looked me over good. Like Mom examines a melon before deciding to buy it or not.

"Wayne on a plaaaaaaaane," he sang. "You have a story."

I shrugged. Story of a nerd.

Do you know how two people who can't talk properly have a conversation?

Answer: In a way that resembles some kind of secret code, that's how.

We waited for the receptionist who looked like 14A to call our names. I tried to smile at her every time I had an appointment. I admit that a sense of guilt washed over me when I saw her. She reminded me that I had ignored 14A. She reminded me that you never knew if the person you were sitting across the aisle from was trying to have the last conversation of her life and would it have hurt you to say something nice about her quilted tree skirt?

So I liked talking to Denny. Denny and I wrote notes. Mostly, Denny wrote questions and I tried to answer them. By the time they called my name for my examination with Dr. P, I'd written out the short but sad biography of Wayne H. Kovok, right down to the plummet to the ground. I showed him Internet photos of the crash. I confided that I was searching for Uncle Reed's flag. It was a relief to tell someone that secret goal.

And Denny sang a secret of his own.

He was terrified of speaking in public, which I could have guessed. But he was about to be forced to speak in public. His bar mitzvah was coming up, and that meant reading out loud in front of his entire synagogue.

Yeah, that is a tough one.

"Do you think God has a sense of humor?" he whispered.

I've never thought about it.

"I do," Denny said. "Why else would he look down on a person with a three-syllable, multivowel name like Rosenblatt and give him a speech impediment? I'll tell you why. Because he likes to laugh."

Maybe.

"People laugh at me all the time. I get shoved into my locker when I talk."

Sorry. I didn't know what else to say. Except that whoever shoved him was a jerk.

"Just try to say Rosenblatt at your next appointment. Just try. I mean, someday Dr. P will pronounce you cured, Wayne. But I'll still stammer in English *and* Hebrew."

I'll still have this scar.

Denny studied me. "But you'll have a cool story about how you got that scar. I'd rather have that."

Did you know "rosen" means "rose" in German? Not a bad name.

"Yeah, I did," he sang. "Do you know how Moses makes his coffee?"

How?

"He*brews* it! Get it?"

Funny.

"I'll tell your grandfather that joke when he comes back from the restroom."

I wouldn't.

Grandpa did not tell jokes. And from what I'd observed my whole life, he didn't get jokes, either.

Denny stammered the joke out, and when he landed the punch line, he had a huge grin on his face.

"I don't get it," Grandpa said.

"Because Moses is Hebrew and he *brews* coffee," Denny explained. Denny attempted to act out the joke by pretending to hold a coffee mug. I should have stopped him, but I was cracking up inside. Watching Grandpa's expression was funnier than any joke.

"I know how to make coffee, son," Grandpa said, then opened his newspaper. I glanced at Grandpa, and he winked at me. An actual wink! Which meant he was yanking Denny's chain. Which was funnier than any joke.

Denny shrugged it off.

Since the accident, I didn't think anyone understood my new language. But writing notes to Denny changed that. I thought he was solid, you know? Someone who would pick me for his Bear Ball team. Or I would pick him first. We would both probably be horrible at Bear Ball, but so what. Misery loves company. We'd be horrible together. The two leftovers.

Twenty-four hours later, I asked Mom if I could go to the mall with Denny after school.

"That's great," Mom said, handing me a wad of cash. "You need to get back to normal. Hop in the car."

You? Drive?

"Yeah, my doctor said I can drive now. Or do you want Grandpa to take you?"

No!

"Do you think Denny would like one of these muffins?"

There was a new basket of Sandy Showalter muffins on the counter. Cranberry orange. Sandy and I were communicating through the giving and receiving of baked goods. Here's how it went. Her mom dropped them off. I texted Sandy.

Dearest Sandy,

Can I compare thee to a lovely poem? Or even to a garden gnome?

Sandy texted back that she hoped I was feeling better. (No mention of how hard it was to find a word that rhymes with *poem*!)

Do you know how many times we had this muffin-to-bad-poetry-text exchange? Six times! That can't be normal.

There are no love songs about baked goods.

I looked it up.

I wrote on my notepad and passed it to Mom: *No muffins for Denny.*

So I put on a baseball cap and let Mom drop me at the mall. At least the cap shaded the L-shaped mark across my face.

"I have to go get something for Grandpa, anyway. Be back in a couple of hours."

What?

"Something for his stomach."

What's wrong?

"He's just rattled, you know. Still worried, I suppose."

No one had told Mom about the Flee's appearance at our door, and I wasn't about to upset her with it. I'd already gotten in trouble *again* for the most recent cheese-burger, which I didn't understand. Grandpa outranked me in every way a person can outrank a seventh grader. How could I stop him from anything?

I found Denny standing where he'd said he'd be. Next to Elegant Engravings, his mother's mall kiosk. It was located directly across from a candle store.

"Heelloooo!" he sang.

"Hi, Wayne," Mrs. Rosenblatt said. "You two have fun."

You spend your time here? I wrote.

And Denny whispered, "What? The entire mall walks past her kiosk every hour. I watch it."

We got my new Adidas pretty fast. The brand-new white rubber soles squeaked on the shiny mall floor.

Squeak. Geek.

Squeak. Geek.

Squeak. Geek.

I had the old Goodwill shoes in a bag. I ditched them in a trash can near the food court. Even though the new shoes made embarrassing squeaks, at least they were one-owner shoes with zero miles on them and no history. They were just waiting to go somewhere new.

Don't call me a complete dork, but that made me feel

great. Like it was a fresh start. New shoes for a new me at a new school. For the first time in weeks, I had hope.

There we were, walking and not talking, but being as normal as a kid with a beat-up face and new shoes and a guy who sing-talks could be.

This is the part of the story where, were I in a horror movie, scary music would warn the audience that something bad was about to happen. Why can't real life come with a sound track? I would like to be warned about potential danger.

Do you know what I considered potential danger?

Sandy Showalter. In person. Sure, I wanted to see *her*, but I wasn't ready to be seen *by* her.

I ducked behind the giant panda standing outside Panda Palace. That panda could hide a soccer team. Denny Rosenblatt followed me behind the panda and sang, "What's wrong?"

I wondered how rude it would be to tell Denny to go away. Not blow my cover. I couldn't do it. I couldn't even write it down. So I just grabbed his sleeve and pulled him away from the food court.

"Wayne!" Denny sang.

I pointed to my eyebrow.

"Ohhhhh!" Denny spun around and scanned the mall.

"You need a disguise," he whispered. "I know the guy at Sunglass Stand. Wait here."

He ran over to Sunglass Stand, a little kiosk fifteen feet from Panda Palace.

I think he tried on every pair. Every pair! He thought he was so hilarious. He tried on Hello Kitty sunglasses. Sunshine sunglasses. Dollar-sign sunglasses. Every stupid kind of sunglasses you could imagine, and he cracked up each time he turned to look at me.

Do you know what kind of sunglasses he brought back to me?

Do you want to know?

Aviators.

Aviators!

Grandpa Dalton aviators.

I should have told him not to get that style. But at least they covered a good part of my face, including two of the three butterfly bandages. I put on the aviators and stepped out from behind the giant panda.

"Wayne?" Sandy Showalter called out. "Is that you?"

Sandy was with a girl with dark hair and a frown to beat all frowns.

I waved back. And then I put my hand up to the place where my left eyebrow used to be. The baseball cap and sunglasses did a good job of hiding it, but the scar going down my cheek was on display. There was no hiding it now. I wished I'd put emu oil on it like Rama had suggested.

Emu oil makes hair grow back faster and scars heal.

I looked it up.

But, you know, I just couldn't get past putting bird grease on my face.

Sandy Showalter had spotted me and that was that. Once again, I had that burning wish that the floor would drop out from underneath me and help me disappear along with my misery.

"Hello," Denny sang.

"So, are you on *American Idol* or something?" Frown Girl asked, and then laughed. And I could see that maybe she was like one of the kids at Denny's school. Kids who shoved him into lockers. And it made me wonder what Sandy was doing with her.

Denny Rosenblatt had the good sense to shrug. The four of us stood there and waited for someone to say something, which normally would have been me, Wayne Kovok, sealing up the cracks of awkward silences.

Did you know that the emu is a flightless bird that looks like a small ostrich? And that, speaking of birds, it's really not accurate to say someone "eats like a bird" if they just nibble at their food? Most birds eat 80 percent of their body weight, so if someone is eating like a bird, they are probably at a buffet.

I waited for Sandy to recoil. I waited for her to give me that look. That Anibal Gomez, *what is wrong with your face* look. It was the longest wait of my life. She took an eternity to scan me.

Do you know what? Her eyes were still as kind as they'd ever been.

Her kindness made me uncomfortable.

Did you know that emus can't fly but are fast runners and eat grasshoppers, caterpillars, and small rodents?

I had the good sense to write Sandy an epic note: Hi.

"Your texts are funny," she replied, smiling.

I'd made her smile. I was still a person who could make Sandy Showalter smile.

Do you know how good that felt? For something like six seconds, I smiled back.

Frown Girl ruined it.

"Who are you and what happened to your face?" Some people are human smile erasers. Frown Girl was one of them.

And you won't believe it, but Denny Rosenblatt launched into song. He sang the brief, recent biography of my life.

"Wayne was on a plane. Wayne was on a plane and the

plane crashed. Oh yeah. It crashed. He was slashed. He survived. Lost his voice. But rejoice! We're looking for it. Yeah. Now he has new Adidas. Don't know if he likes fajitas."

True story.

I'm telling you that the singing didn't bother me too much. He got the facts out pretty well. He got it out faster than I could have written it down on my notepad.

Frown Girl said to Sandy, "I'm going to get a Coke. Text me when you're done."

What bothered me was the sudden realization that Sandy Showalter's friend didn't know who I was. And if she didn't know who I was, sort-of-boyfriend to Sandy at most, receiver of sympathy muffins at least, then that was because Sandy hadn't told her. And I knew Sandy talked to other girls. She was the one who'd told Mysti and Rama that I could call her. Yes, I was no girl expert, but I knew a little bit about how girls operated behind the scenes.

Was I kidding myself? Were the muffins just orbs of baked pity?

I wanted to sprint Jesse Owens–style out of the mall. I stood speechless in front of Sandy Showalter with my heart suddenly pounding and my deodorant failing.

Did you know the emu is believed to be a survivor of prehistoric times and their eggs are emerald green?

"I'm doing horrible in Spanish," Sandy said.

157

Did you know that emus are strong swimmers?

"Want a Dr Pepper?" she asked.

She headed toward the food court, and when I remembered I had feet, I moved, too.

No one cares about stupid emu facts, Wayne!

My stupid new shoes squeaked against the shiny mall floor. And all I heard echoing in my head was

Geek.

Geek.

Geek.

Sandy got tired of me after just three slurps of Dr Pepper.

"Gotta go. My mom's waiting for us! Bye!" she said.

I knew what that meant. I knew girl-speak for *This is lame.*

Maybe I should have retreated right then, but I didn't. I stayed and watched the back of her head and that perfect golden hair of hers disappear into the crowd. I locked the image of her smile in my brain, though.

Denny and I trolled the mall together, and I tried to step on my toes so that my shoes wouldn't herald my geekdom.

"I shouldn't have started singing. It was dumb."

It wasn't dumb.

"I feel stupid."

Let's go back to your mom's store.

"Let's keep walking," he whispered.

No more walking.

"Come on," Denny said.

We found a bench outside a store called Claire's, which Denny called a "target-rich" environment of girls he could never talk to. But I wasn't looking at anything but my superbright shoes. I thought about how nice it would be to run down my block in these new shoes. How I needed to run again. Maybe in the middle of the night like I did on New Year's. When the streets were all mine.

Denny whispered, "Next up, Sears."

Why?

"Miserable girls."

Denny had a way to put a thousand questions in my brain (who wants to look at miserable girls and why are they in Sears?) and answer each one just as fast (many girls are dragged to the mall against their will on a dad errand).

Denny said that finding a pretty girl in Sears was a gold mine. Her misery made her more beautiful because she was out of place, standing around all those tools and tires. Denny said it was like spotting a rare bird at a landfill.

Which, after I thought about it, sounded pretty good to me. I decided I might be able to learn a thing or three from Denny Rosenblatt.

You spend a lot of time here?

"I practically grew up here," he whispered.

So we trudged to Sears to test out Denny's theory. We moved through the rows of power drills and toolboxes in search of loveliness.

True story.

And doggone it if Denny wasn't right.

A girl with a long brown braid and a red-and-blue flannel shirt trailed behind a male parental unit.

"But, Dad, when can I get my phone back?" she whined.

She looked completely out of place and full of misery.

Beautiful misery.

Denny rounded the corner and walked right in front of the Sears girl.

And he sang, "If you want to find a rare beauty out of school, look in the store where you can buy a tool."

And the girl did some eyebrow gymnastics at first, but then she broke into a laugh. I stepped up behind Denny and shrugged at the girl, then pulled him away.

"See what I mean, Wayne on a plane," Denny sang. "A beautiful creature out of its element is even more beautiful. Even if I can't talk to her."

If a pretty girl is spotted in an unsearched area of the mall, then how many fallen objects may be found in unsearched areas of East Texas? That was the path my brain chose to take.

Fact: I ended the day with three new things. New

shoes, a new friend, and a new theory about unsearched areas of Texas.

DATA

New debris found.

A one-pound biography of Steve Jobs was found in the yard of one Thomas Flint near Route 69 between Jefferson and Karnack, Texas.

Fact highlighted on Texas map—Thomas Flint lives two miles farther east of established debris field.

The Steve Jobs biography and the American flag exited Flight 56 at approximately the same minute.

Debris field widens to seventeen miles.

Notes: Unpopulated areas of East Texas just beyond crash site have yielded zero reported debris. Potential unsearched debris field.

Extend search area east toward Caddo Lake State Park, potential Sears of investigation.

CHAPTER 16

Ever since Denny and I spotted the beautiful miserable girl in Sears, I couldn't stop thinking about unsearched geography. I couldn't stop thinking that unsearched geography was the key to solving the mystery of the missing flag. It was still out there. I was sure of it. Why not. Did you know that people were still finding debris from the tragic *Columbia* space shuttle disaster? Back in 2003, that shuttle broke up over East Texas, too. The debris field stretched over hundreds of square miles. Investigators and searchers found about eighty-four thousand pieces of debris (only 39 percent of the shuttle's total weight) early in the investigation. But people are *still* finding debris. Someone found one of the doomed shuttle's tanks on a lake bed *eight years* after the disaster. So my hypothesis was that people in East Texas were still looking for debris. And maybe they'd stumble upon our flag. Do you know how hopeful that made me?

The inside of my closet door was fast becoming covered with maps. I had just shown them to Denny, and he was the only other person on the planet who knew about them. A map of all the areas the NTSB had searched. Red pins denoted searched areas, and yellow pins indicated sites where East Texas residents had reported debris near their barns. The maximum distance an object was located from the crash site was still within a seventeen-mile radius. What was beyond that radius?

As I considered this theory, my phone buzzed.

Was it a message from Liz Delaney?

No.

It was Sandy.

Mom won't let me break up with W!!!! Says it wud b cruel 2 do right now, which is true??

Then she wrote back to me in a hurry:

Wayne, my kid sister was playing with my phone. Ha ha! How r u?

How was I? Well, I was in the know.

That's how I was.

What I wanted to reply: *Please listen to your mom!*

What I did reply:

Hi. ☺

I know. I know. No one would ever accuse Wayne Kovok of being Shakespeare.

"Hey, open up, soldier. New muffins have arrived via Sandy's mother," Grandpa said through my closed door. "I've been alerted that I need to check with you if I want to consume them."

I shot a look at Denny.

I closed the closet door before Grandpa could see. He was in the hallway, already consuming a muffin.

I gave him a quick thumbs-up.

"Why are you wearing sunglasses indoors?" he asked. This was sort of a stupid question considering he was wearing *his* sunglasses indoors at that exact moment. I could see my reflection in them.

I shrugged. When you don't have a voice, you appreciate the economy of the shrug. It communicates *I don't care, I don't know,* or *maybe* in one convenient gesture, and those were all the feelings I had about sunglasses and muffins. I squeezed past Grandpa and went to the kitchen.

A white basket of blueberry muffins mocked my feelings for the most beautiful girl in the world. They were a baked reminder of plane wreckage and Wayne-and-Sandy wreckage.

I might have destroyed a blueberry muffin.

Okay, I destroyed a blueberry muffin.

I squeezed it into pieces. Mr. Darcy ran over to gobble it up off the floor.

Denny tried to whisper to me, "It's okay."

Then I went into the living room. Being equidistant from my room, which held my cell phone, and the kitchen, which had pity muffins, it seemed like the only safe place in the house.

"Sergeant, just go ahead and give the man his coup de grâce!" Grandpa shouted at the TV. Muffin crumbs dribbled from his hand.

What? I wrote and pushed the note in front of his face.

"What? A coup de grâce? That's a death blow intended to end the suffering of a wounded man. Now, stop talking over this movie, W!"

I tried hard to concentrate on the military movie. I'd noticed lately that if I sat very quietly with Grandpa while he was watching a show, he would talk to me. More accurately, he would point things out and I would nod.

It was the closest thing we had to normal conversation. And to tell you the truth, I was starting to get used to it. To enjoy it a little. Grandpa had a ton of cool facts in his brain.

"Hey, Wayne, if you get a chance, tell your girlfriend you want bran muffins next. Keeps your morning constitutional regular. You know what I'm saying, right?"

Grandpa had mentioned his morning constitutional once before. I thought it had to do with something patriotic. It doesn't. It means your first visit to the bathroom.

I looked it up.

I nodded to him about the muffins and pretended to watch the TV. But my brain kept saying, *Wayne, you're not stupid. You know who Sandy's other friend with a W is. They've been friends since the fourth grade.*

Wendy.

Wayne.

W.

The wrong *W* in a list of phone contacts.

Was it just me, or was the accidental text the likely deathblow of many a relationship?

Denny whispered to me, "You need unbiased girl confirmation. Maybe it doesn't mean what you think it means."

Where could I get unbiased girl confirmation?

I ran down the hall, grabbed my phone, and sent a text message of my own. I texted my old friends Mysti and Rama and told them the whole story in three spare sentences.

After thirty minutes, they texted back. (I figured they used that space of thirty minutes to call each other and discuss my coup de grâce.)

So sorry, Wayne.

That was their studied answer.

"So sorry, Wayne on a plane," Denny sang.

In my brain, I filed a new scientific method report. I pictured the report morphing into a science-fair display board with bright, bold lettering on a table in the Beatty Middle School library.

Question: What happens to a boy with a beat-up face and no voice when he gets an accidental breakup message from the girl of his dreams?

Hypothesis: The boy will do nothing about it.

Procedure: Epic denial of misfired text.

Probable conclusion: When Wayne Kovok regains his voice, he will lose his sort-of-boyfriend status.

New topic.

Denny, did you know that Minecraft was

167

originally called the Cave Game and that the Creeper started out as a coding error?

"You were like this before the crash, right?" Denny asked.

Pretty much.

"Except you could eat french fries and tacos."

Yeah. Except I had an uncle and a sort-of girlfriend, went to a normal school, and didn't share a bathroom with my grandpa. Except for those things, I was mostly the same.

DATA

Items still missing in the world:

• *Possible treasure buried beneath the Alamo, known as the San Saba treasure believed to have been buried by the Texas defenders.*

• *The fortune of 1930s mobster Dutch Schultz, which vanished without a trace*

• *Part of Montezuma's treasure rumored to have been stored in Utah.*

• *The Amber Room: An entire room that went missing. Made with elaborate amber panels and gold-leaf mirrors in the eighteenth century, given to Russia's Peter the Great. Later disassembled by the Nazis and taken to Königsberg Castle, never to be seen again.*

• *Spartacus, whose body was never found*

• *Amelia Earhart, aviator who disappeared in 1937 while trying to fly solo around the world*

CHAPTER 17

Twenty-four hours had passed since the nightmare of the mis-sent text.

But there was some good news.

I'd just come from Dr. P.

"The swelling around your vocal cords has significantly decreased," he said. "I don't expect permanent damage, so you can resume dreaming of being a famous rock star."

I raised my good eyebrow. Once I had invented a group called Epic Scientists, but had only gotten as far as writing the title for a hit song. It was called "The Data Says You Like Me."

True story.

But I never really had the dream of becoming a rock star.

He said if I kept up my therapy, I should expect fast results.

"You should expect fast results," Dr. P said. "Probably be saying my name out loud in four to five weeks if you keep up with your exercises. You might also be able to start eating more solid foods."

So that was good news.

But also bad news. Sandy would let me go as soon as I could speak. I knew that. I even understood it. But I didn't want to accept it.

I decided to distract myself by working on math. Yes, I know that's sort of lame: forgetting a girl by doing something mathematical. But here's another weird story Uncle Reed once told me. There's a technique they teach Special Forces soldiers to employ when they're under intense questioning. It's thought that if you run the multiplication tables in your head while answering a question, you can beat a lie detector test. So why not apply that method to forgetting about anything?

It worked.

It worked really great. I started looking up facts about multiplication. Then I just couldn't help but do more research on strange flights and missing objects. The more I researched, the less the falling sensation took hold of my body. It was a good strategy. I logged hours of computer-screen therapy. I forgot about the missing flag for a little while, too.

It was a great distraction until I found something new to worry about.

Did you know that one new worry can cancel out one old one?

Now, Grandpa didn't know how to efficiently use the computer. Nope. Not at all. He might have been super smart about rifles and reconnaissance and how to drill patriotism into new recruits, but he knew nothing about how to close out computer programs. Every time I used the computer after he'd been on it, I'd find about fifty windows open, sucking up all the computer memory. He did this all the time.

All. The. Time.

Even before he lived here, he'd come over and work on our computer.

Yours just works better. Mine's too slow, he'd say, and I'd think, *Yeah, because you have fifty windows open. Don't they teach you that in the army?*

But I liked to spy on Grandpa's search history.

Weather sites. Old-car rallies. The best kind of food for a turtle. Balms for joint ache. Climate-change conspiracy theories. You never knew what you were going to find with him. Back when I had a voice, I could go look at his computer history and sneak it into a sentence to get him worked up.

For example, *My science teacher said old cars are damaging our environment and could be linked to climate change.*

The face. The Grandpa face. A mix of frustration and grumpiness and *I'm gonna tell you, kid* all in one. I used to love getting him to make that face. I had to laugh on the inside. Any outside laughing was cause for a push-up challenge.

So you think you're funny, do you, Kovok? Well, I can still beat you at push-ups! Drop and do twenty, he'd order.

And I'd have to drop right there and do twenty push-ups. By the time I was on push-up number fifteen, he'd be done and standing over me. *Who's laughing now, Kovok?*

True story.

So I sat down in front of our computer and snooped at his open windows.

The first window: Baylor Liver and Pancreas Disease Center.

The second window: Willowbend Health and Wellness.

Third: Dr. Lisell, oncologist.

And it went on and on.

Articles about the pancreas. Best foods for pancreatic cancer patients. Best treatments. Best prognoses.

With each window I scanned, I tried to follow what I read. Connect it to Grandpa.

I didn't like the associations my brain made. It formed a mind map like one of those school analogy assignments where you draw a line across the page from one word to another.

Apple—Fruit
Shoe—Foot
Stomach problems—Grandpa
Grandpa—Cancer

I pushed away from the keyboard like it was suddenly toxic. Dangerous. Like I understood too much, too fast.

"What are you doing?" Grandpa's sudden ninja-like presence never stopped surprising me.

I spun around lightning fast and there he was, holding a coffee mug, wearing his aviator sunglasses, smiling. Smiling either because he scared me or he caught me. He wore that *you need to drop and do push-ups* face, too. I figured he'd caught me.

"What are you staring at?"

Shrug.

"You've got a question, Wayne, let it out."

I had lots of questions. But it wasn't like any of them were going to push themselves out of my "significantly improved" throat.

"Your mother's home, so go help her with the groceries," he commanded.

In the kitchen, Mom boiled water for pasta. I rearranged the blue glass birds back into circle formation. Then I made my dinner smoothie.

I wrote a note: *Set out two plates?*

Maybe a change in Grandpa's diet would reveal a clue.

"Yes. Two."

That didn't give me any data. He wasn't eating anything different from Mom.

"How is your friend Denny?"

Good.

"That's good. I'm glad you've made a new friend. New friends are important, don't you think?"

Important. Sure.

"I might have a new friend, too. How would you feel if I went on a date with a new friend?"

I found myself double shocked. First I find out my grandpa might be sick. Right when he's not the most annoying houseguest ever. And second, my mom is querying me about a date. My mom dating? Let's just say that rarely happens. She is super picky. as she should be.

I wrote on my notepad: *Who?*

"His name is Tim LeMoot. And why are you wearing

those sunglasses to the dinner table? You look like you're spying on me."

Wait, Tim LeMoot, the Texas Boot?

"Yes."

The TV lawyer guy?

"Yes."

Tim LeMoot! TIM LEMOOT! Tim LeMoot who screams through our TV?

"Yes, Wayne, that's the guy."

What??? Why??

"Well, we have a lot in common."

After your money?

"No, nothing like that."

Facts: Tim LeMoot, the Texas Boot, is that accident-injury attorney, and my mom has recently been in an accident.

Smelled like a bad idea.

"I know what you're thinking. That it's a bad idea. But he's a human being. He happened to graduate from Southern Methodist University and has a thirteen-year-old daughter named Debra. He likes to play Ping-Pong, and he also sails on White Rock Lake."

I looked at her bug-eyed and she said, "I anticipated your interrogation, Wayne, so I thought I'd just go ahead and give you his biography."

I wrote: *Does he like Jane Austen movies?*

It was doubtful he did.

"Well, I don't know. Why?"

And I wrote: *Because YOU do. Important!*

"Look, the truth is that we went out a couple of times before the accident, so ..."

Oh.

What was I going to say to my mother about dating, huh? That was a place I didn't want to go. It made me feel nauseated just thinking about it. Tim LeMoot. The Texas Boot. No way was that a good idea.

Was he the friend who gave you advice about the airline thing?

"Well, yes."

Later, we sat at the dinner table, and Mom and Grandpa ate plain buttered pasta while I drank what felt like my millionth fruit smoothie. Nobody talked. The forks made a racket and you could hear every slurp of the straw. If Hank Williams had been in the room, I bet you could have heard the crunch of lettuce between his jaws.

I studied the two of them. They held their forks the exact same way. They spun the pasta around their forks three times. They unfolded their napkins the exact same way. They probably kept their secrets about illnesses the same way, too.

Now, because I didn't know if either of them talked to each other about cancer or dating, I decided to make the dinner conversation a little more interesting.

So I passed a note to Grandpa: *Mom's going on a date with the Texas Boot.*

"Can't be worse than Mr. Medieval," Grandpa said, shoveling a forkful of pasta into his mouth.

I'd forgotten all about Mr. Medieval.

Mr. Medieval was a jousting trainer for the Medieval Times restaurant, and if you think I'm a nerd with facts, well, at least I spread around the topics a bit. Mr. Medieval was a two-topic guy: jousting and himself.

You, lad, may call me Sir Mike, he'd said when we went to see his show. And then he kept referring to himself in the third person. *Sir Mike thinks that you would make a good serf. Sir Mike has reserved seats for you at the seven thirty showing. Sir Mike will show the lady to her table. Sir Mike would like to challenge you to a duel.*

And I always thought, *Sir Mike should lose our phone number.*

Eventually, he did.

"Oh, Wayne, your dad called. He can't make it this weekend."

That made three weekends in a row. I guess Grandpa scared him off good. Or maybe he was still mad that I

hadn't gone with him to see about our case. I still hadn't
asked Mom what all that was about.

Dinner ended with lots of ice cream and no more talk
about Mom dating.

I'm going to the park.

"Take your phone," Mom said.

I grabbed my skateboard and set out down Cedar
Drive. The sky was full of heavy gray-blue clouds. A storm
was coming. You could smell it in the air. I got to the park
and walked to a clearing where there weren't any trees to
obstruct my view of the sky. I lay down and watched the
sky. The planes crossing. The flashes of light. The sound of
distant thunder mixed with the metal-whistling sound of
planes slicing the air. The jets—a stream of fast-moving
air. I'd gotten to know all their sounds now. I could support a plane for sixty seconds over the park before it disappeared behind the tall cottonwood trees. I prayed the
storm would do nothing but rain. The planes would all
arrive safe. Happy.

Tonight, 14A was a Chinese exchange student who
listened to music.

Another plane carried an entire family to California,
where they were going to see the ocean for the first time.

The last plane was just like my old school bus. Carl the
bus driver was now Carl the pilot. The rows of seats were

filled with kids from Beatty. The plane headed toward the water tower. So I raced home on my skateboard and watched it fly on. I got inside the house just before the rain hit.

Later, I went to bed, my head all mixed up. I called Mr. Darcy into my room and talked to him in an inaudible whisper. I'd been getting good at just mouthing words to Mr. Darcy.

You know what makes you forget to remember the girl of your dreams or beat-up faces or unfound flags?

Mr. Darcy had no answer.

The fact that your grandfather might be sick just when you were starting to get used to him being around, that's what. Just when you were counting on him being there.

Just makes you want to give life a high five, doesn't it?

Or a punch in the face.

Why? Why? Why?

Hours later, I couldn't sleep. The rain had come and gone. So I decided to sneak outside for a run.

I told myself I'm still a sort-of boyfriend because Sandy thinks I believed her little sister sent that text. And she doesn't know I'm starting to make vowel sounds in Dr. P's office. And Grandpa? He's just doing research. Mom's going out with the Texas Boot and I've got leads on the missing American flag. It's just out there waiting for me to find it, and as soon as I do, everything will be fine.

Everything was fine.

Everything was probably fine.

I grabbed my Adidas from the space next to the front door.

"Couldn't sleep, either, huh?" It was Grandpa and I was busted.

I shook my head.

"You take your phone when you go running, don't you?" He knew.

I nodded.

"Good. Safer that way. Stay alert."

There was no topic I could scribble. No notepad to scribble it on.

"Hey, now that I think about it, mind if I run with you?"

I smiled. *Absolutely!*

"Okay, let me get my shoes on."

We got outside and he stretched a little.

Grandpa set out running in the direction of the bus stop, and I trailed behind him. Across the street, the big white Christmas snowman was *still* out in my neighbors' front yard. Only it was flat and deflated and weighed down with rainwater. I remembered that decoration. Back in December, when it was inflated, it had two outstretched arms and looked like it wanted to hug you. Now it merely looked like it had surrendered, fallen forward, and melted. And it made me wonder what my neighbors were waiting for and why they couldn't just put the stupid snowman away.

"Step up your pace, Kovok!"

I put my hands up in the air. I tried to communicate *Where? What?*

"We're running until I get tired, and I'm not tired yet."

Good, I told myself. *Don't get tired. Keep running. Sick people don't run, do they? Healthy people run. Grandpa is healthy. Very healthy.*

I prayed that was a fact, not just a wish.

DATA

Wind-speed performance:

• *Zero miles per hour = still air and no movement*

• *1–3 miles per hour = leaves rustle, minimal kite movement*

• *4–7 miles per hour = wind felt on face, flags flap gently*

• 8–12 miles per hour = wind felt on face

• 17–21 miles per hour = small trees sway

• 22–27 miles per hour = tree branches move, wires whistle, land kites

• 28–33 miles per hour = strong winds, whole trees in motion

• 48–55 miles per hour = trees uprooted, structural damage likely

Wind speed on date of crash: 50-plus miles per hour

Question: If a 4-pound cotton object with the dimensions 5 feet by 9.5 feet goes aloft at 30,000 feet, flying 500 miles per hour, does it have the power to land at a distance greater than 17 miles from the crash site?

Hypothesis: A kite-like object weighing four pounds has greater wind surface and less downdraft than the typical suitcase; therefore, it would travel farther eastward.

CHAPTER 18

It was a week later and I was at Denny's house, using his computer for some stealth searching. He sang, "Maybe you should let it go. Small flag. Large space. It's like trying to find a needle in a haystack. Stop worrying about it. Order a new flag, maybe? Liz Delaney isn't going to write you back."

You would think that Denny's cool singing voice would soften the blow, somehow. But it stuck in my mind like a bad commercial jingle. Reality doesn't sound any better in song form.

True story.

He still kept singing.

"Liz Delaney isn't going to write you back. It's like a needle in a haystack."

I was beginning to believe only Mr. Darcy truly understood me.

Did you know a family received an army soldier's medals thirty years after they went missing?

Denny motioned for me to keep writing.

He was a Green Beret in Vietnam and had earned a ton of medals. And they were to be returned to his family after his funeral, but there was some confusion and they went missing for a long time. Then his family got the call and they were delivered. Thirty years later.

"So you're saying it's possible that lost things can be found?" Denny whispered.

Exactly!

I told him about my research on the *Columbia* space shuttle and how debris was still being found.

"So you will find the flag, then, or someone like Liz Delaney will find it? Or some other mystery person?" Denny asked.

Yes.

"It's a good theory," Denny said.

It's a great theory.

"I wish I had your problems, Wayne on a plane," Denny whispered. He suddenly looked depressed.

What?

185

"I wish I could be on a search for something lost, but I can't," Denny sang, pacing around his room as he did. "I, Dennis Rosenblatt, have to read out loud in front of an entire synagogue. *Out loud!*"

Sorry.

"Yeah. Be sure to get a front-row seat. It's going to be hilarious," he whispered.

"Okay, boys, ready for dinner?" It was Mrs. Rosenblatt at the door to Denny's room, smiling, wearing an apron that read KISS THE COOK. Mrs. Rosenblatt was nice. So nice that last week she had to do that mom thing and try to touch my beat-up face and I had to recoil and write *Hurts* on my notepad. The truth? My face didn't hurt as much.

"Mashed potatoes for you, Wayne," Mrs. Rosenblatt said. "As soon as you are all healed, I'm going to make you an ambitious sandwich that you will never forget. Roast chicken. Swiss cheese. Tomatoes. Lettuce. The works. Don't I make the best sandwiches, Denny?"

"Yes," Denny said. "The best sandwich ever."

If there were a contest for torturing someone's taste buds, the Rosenblatts would win.

Still, she gave me a nice bowl of delicious mashed potatoes. That eased the agony of not being able to eat the best sandwich ever.

So I sat at the Rosenblatt family dinner table while

everyone passed around dishes of delicious food. Denny had a loud house. There were at least five conversations going on at once among Denny, his father, his smiling mother, his aunt Sheila, and his little brother and sister. Especially Mrs. Rosenblatt. The way she talked made up for any nontalkers at the table.

"Denny, set the table, kids, don't climb on that, did you see that article about food preservatives, Sheila, I can't shop there anymore, put the dishes in the dishwasher, no, I never said it was broken, I said it just doesn't work, there's a difference."

I watched them pass their plates while Denny's mother told everyone what to do and asked him about fifteen times if he'd practiced his reading.

"Let the boy eat," Denny's dad said.

"We are so proud of Denny," Mrs. Rosenblatt said. "Wayne, he is going to wear his great-grandfather's prayer shawl that all the Rosenblatt men have worn for their bar mitzvahs. Did you know that?"

Nope, didn't know that.

And did I know that Denny needed to practice reading his Torah portion?

And did I know that after Denny got up in front of everyone, and the service was completed, he would be considered a man?

"We can't wait to hear him read," Mrs. Rosenblatt said.

Denny got real interested in his meat loaf, and why wouldn't he? Everyone was focused on how nice it would be to hear him read out loud.

Out loud!

Man, what was his family thinking? It seemed obvious to me that a kid like Denny would be too terrified to read a grocery list to a crowd, much less ancient Hebrew. Didn't the Rosenblatts see the elephant in their dining room?

Denny turned to me, took my pad of paper, and sent me an SOS signal using Morse code.

··· — — — ···

And I wrote back, Did you know that people are wrong when they say the distress signal SOS stands for Save Our Ship? It doesn't stand for anything. S-O-S was created in 1906 because it had nine keystrokes—three dots, three dashes, three dots— and was the easiest Morse code combination to transmit.

Sandy Showalter's middle name was Olivia.

It's ironic that the girl who plagued me would have the initials SOS.

Ironic with a capital I.

I should have known better than to crush on a girl with those initials.

Denny wrote: You're a nerd!

I know!

Just when you think you've got a messed-up situation and more questions than answers, you sit at a big wooden table with a bunch of hungry, talking Rosenblatts and realize that Denny Rosenblatt would, in fact, love to trade places with someone searching for a red, white, and blue cloth rather than face the fear of reading in front of a hundred people. So over a meat loaf dinner, I realized something.

I was plagued.

But Denny was plagued, too.

Maybe we all were.

CHAPTER 19

Did you know that rats are strong enough to bite through a toenail?

Rats.

Stinking rats. They can wiggle into a space as small as a quarter, so look around your house and make sure you don't have any rat crevices or long toenails. It's a good thing we all don't live in New York City, where there're supposed to be two million stinking rats. Or in Africa, where the Gambian pouched rat grows up to fifteen pounds.

Even I could be grossed out by that fact.

I might be grossed out by that fact.

Okay, I was officially grossed out by that fact.

A fifteen-pound rat that can bite through a toenail is gross.

But you know what? It made me calm down to think of Sandy being grossed out by that fact, too. I used to love causing girls to do that pinched-up, gross-out face in fifth grade. A solid gross fact is the best girl repellent in the universe.

True story.

Okay, so, rats. Rats like to eat dog food. We kept Mr. Darcy's dog food in the garage in a large plastic container. Last week, some stinking rat chewed a hole in the bucket, and Grandpa went ballistic because, you know, that meant a rat dared to be within a one-mile radius of the Car.

"Wayne, you have rat traps around here?"

No, sir.

The next day, a big box of rat traps appeared on our kitchen counter.

"Would you mind setting these up after school and getting this problem taken care of?"

Sure.

I would be useful. How hard could it be?

As soon as Grandpa drove me home from school, he got sick from his mystery illness that made him barf up burgers and the sandwich from Mrs. Rosenblatt (yes, she sent one home with me anyway). So I set up two rat traps, which is an easy enough task if you research "Rat Traps + Best Results" online. You put peanut butter on the lever and a nugget of dog food on the trap just to attract the rat. Then you leave the trap up next to a wall because, like all rodents, rats like to travel along a wall line.

I set the trap along the garage wall and another one on the outside wall next to the patio. I figured getting the stinking rat coming or going was a good plan. Then I went to my room to do boring reading homework from my new school.

Later, I went to the kitchen to make a smoothie, and that was when I heard it.

Snap! Pop! Ka-BANG!

And I thought, *Man, I nailed that stinking rat already. See if he messes with Mr. Darcy's food again! High five, Wayne Kovok! Grandpa's going to love this.*

Well, it wasn't the rat.

Nope. Not a rat.

It was a blue jay.

A blue jay. A blue jay with one leg, bleeding bird blood all over the patio. And it will sound weird, but I thought of Sandy sitting there in language arts class talking about some stupid poem I couldn't figure out, her long, smooth hair moving back and forth because she was so excited about whatever it was we were supposed to be learning. And I envied her for being that way. (I only got that worked up about a subject if it was science or

Texas history.) The poem Sandy went crazy for had used the word *bewildered*, which is not a word you hear every day. In fact, I'd never heard it before, and it stuck in my brain.

I guess I liked the word all right, but I never understood what it was to actually be bewildered.

Until the stupid blue jay nabbed the dog-food nugget and got stuck in the trap. Man, that made me feel all kinds of bewildered. I didn't know what to do, and I just stood there and thought about my options while the blue jay stood on one leg and bled and waited for me to make a decision. It stared at me, tried to yoga balance, and *poof!* Lights-out! It flopped over dead.

I felt lower than a gopher hole.

"What in tarnation is this?" Grandpa said.

I shrugged. I wasn't going to write the whole Greek tragedy on my notepad.

Boy Murders Bird and Vows Rat Revenge.

"You killed a bird with a rat trap?" Grandpa laughed, then punched me on the shoulder. Hard. "A bird? I've never even heard of that."

I hadn't ever heard of this happening, either. My neck went red from embarrassment. Just when I thought I could relax around him, not feel useless every ten seconds, this had to happen.

I made a mental note to ask Mom when he was going to move back home. Being useless around Grandpa was exhausting.

I went inside to get a bag and put the blue jay in it and carried it out to the trash. And Grandpa stood planted on the patio, still having a great laugh and shouting into the trees, "You birds better whistle and watch out. Wayne here's got it in for you."

The bird blood had sunk into the patio, and it took some doing with bleach to get it out. I wasn't going to have any evidence lying around for me to remember or for the old man to relive my humiliation.

And then he said, "Wait until I tell Reed about this. Ha!"

I froze. The world froze.

His smile vanished. Our eyes locked, and I wondered which way Grandpa was going to go. Left or right. The all-riled-up, patriotic-and-have-a-memorial-moment Grandpa. Or the deflated, *I just now remembered that my hero son is gone* Grandpa.

He had the second kind of moment.

Everything went to fuzz. Slow minus the motion.

His hand wobbled, and he dropped his coffee mug. It shattered and splattered all over the patio where I'd been cleaning up the bird. Only it wasn't coffee, I could tell, because it smelled sweet like tea. The fumes of bleach and sadness and tea nearly flattened me.

And Grandpa stood there still as stone. It was horrible. "Got a broom?" he asked.

I nodded and went inside for the broom and dustpan. I cleaned it all up while Grandpa went to the living room and watched TV. I threw away the shards of the mug in the kitchen trash. There on the counter was a box of tea.

Herbal, caffeine-free tea. No coffee.

Was this unspoken proof of illness? Grandpa hated tea. He called tea drinkers sissies.

A hard, painful knot formed in my throat where my voice was supposed to be. I swallowed. Pain shot up through my neck, and tears tried their best to push their way out, but I stuffed them down.

Stupid rat.

Stupid bird.

Stupid random bird!

My stomach lurched. It's silly, maybe even stupid, okay, but it killed me that something else had fallen from the sky on my watch.

And it's going to sound stupid, but I guess I knew how that blue jay felt when the spring on the trap closed on its leg. Like a person boarding a plane and thinking it will land, safe and normal, then smack, you're in a daze and beat up and living with a sad mom and her sad dad. And you survived and others didn't and you have no idea how or why.

Why? Why? Why?

It is the question that will plague you.

Bewildering.

There was no other word for it on the planet.

It was bewildering.

DATA

Data that might affect location of the flag:

• *Air temperature on date of crash: low 50s.*

• *Winds: out of the south at 50 miles per hour, wind speed that moves whole trees. The National Weather Service defines a severe thunderstorm as having wind speeds of 58 miles per hour or higher.*

• *Precrash weather report. Source: AccuWeather. Damaging thunderstorms and travel disruptions due to high-winds prediction. Cities impacted: Houston, Texas; Shreveport, Louisiana; Jackson, Mississippi;*

New Orleans, Louisiana. Risk of tornadoes within this zone on Saturday after dark.

Supporting Evidence:

• *Meteorologist quote: "My concern is that since this storm is both out of season and on a holiday travel weekend, people might be caught off guard."*

CHAPTER 20

It was Friday night and Mom had a date with Tim LeMoot, the Texas Boot.

Denny had texted me: Provide pictorial evidence and let me know if LeMoot wears black cowboy boots on a date.

I spied him as he came up our front walk. To me, LeMoot looked like he'd walked right out of his own commercial. Shiny gray suit. Slicked-back hair. And black cowboy boots. He held pink flowers in his hands and rang the doorbell.

He said, "Hi, Jennifer, how do you feel about Italian food?"

I didn't know about Mom, but I, Wayne Kovok, had *lots* of feelings about food.

Lots.

My feelings were that I missed food. I dreamed about food. I had to leave the room when certain foods were around. It felt like food was an ex-girlfriend I couldn't talk to anymore without drooling.

So yeah, I had food *feelings*.

The Boot smiled at Mom with his *Call me NOW, I'm waiting* smile. She had done her hair in a way that covered the left side of her face to disguise her missing eyebrow. She had to keep her head tilted so that her hair would fall across the empty space. (I wondered how she was going to pull that off all night.)

There was no sales pitch at all from LeMoot. No TV-volume voice. No *I'll kick money in your wallet* kind of stuff. Still, I worried that he might be a loser. So what if they'd dated before the accident? He might be a rat. Well, maybe that was an unfortunate choice of words considering my recent rat debacle.

"Thanks for the flowers," Mom said. "I'll put them in some water." She let him stand there in the entryway on the YOU ARE HERE rug. All of a sudden, that rug embarrassed the beans out of me, so I waited in the kitchen. You can see right to the front door from where our kitchen sink is, so I pretended to wipe down the counter so that I could keep an eye on the Texas Boot.

Tim LeMoot said, "Nice little place you got here."

As Mom arranged the pink flowers, I shoved a note in front of her: MONEY IN YOUR WALLET RIGHT NOW!

"Wayne, shush."

"Is that your son in there?" Tim LeMoot said.

"Wayne, this is Tim LeMoot," Mom said.

"Nice to meet you, Wayne." He held out his hand to shake mine. I didn't want to touch the Texas Boot, but I did anyway because I knew Mom would pinch me later. Grandpa barreled into the kitchen and went straight to the teapot.

"How do, sir?" Tim LeMoot said to Grandpa.

Tim LeMoot tried to shake Grandpa's hand, too. Grandpa held his mug like a shield. Then he walked back to the big chair in the living room.

"Well, all right. How about we head out?" Tim LeMoot said. He rubbed his palms together and then smoothed his suit, which didn't need smoothing. He spun around on his boot heel so fast that one of his arms knocked the vase of pink flowers right off the counter.

"Oh, sorry, sorry, sorry," he said. "So sorry."

"It's okay," Mom said.

"I'll get you more," the Boot said. "Flowers, I mean. Flowers."

Mom smiled her pretty smile at him.

It was weird that LeMoot was nervous. I hadn't expected that at all. So I snapped a quick picture of him as he knelt down to collect the vase and the flowers. I knew Denny would love that. Maybe the Texas Boot wasn't going to be all bad. Maybe it was about time that Mom was happy, too.

But as the Boot and Mom headed out the front door to go eat Italian food, you know who was outside, tapping his shoe on the sidewalk?

The Flee.

"What in the name of Sam Hill are you doing here, Doug?" Mom asked.

"I'm returning your call," the Flee said. I kept the front door cracked open so that I could hear what they were saying.

"You return calls via the phone," she said.

"Well, this one is an in-person response," he said. "You were supposed to consult with me before making the airline decision."

"No, not really," she answered. "And stop acting like this all happened to you. It didn't. The accident happened to me and your son. I think we can pretty well make up our own minds."

"But Stephanie's dad says—"

She cut him off. "I don't care what Stephanie's dad says."

I noticed the Boot standing there, wondering what was going on. And then I wasn't just embarrassed about the rug in our entry. I was embarrassed all the way to the front curb.

"Mind if I ask who this is?" Tim LeMoot asked.

"This is Wayne's father, Doug Kovok," she said. "Doug, this is Tim LeMoot."

"I know who this fancy-pants lawyer is," the Flee said.

Mom twisted her hair, exposing her missing eyebrow.

"It's time for you to go, Doug," Mom said.

"I have business with my son," the Flee said. "I got him a concert T-shirt." It was then that I saw he had a shirt in his hand.

"I'll give it to him," Mom said.

The Flee stood out there in his faded Beatles T-shirt. He looked like a kid who'd gotten called to the office. And Tim LeMoot, in his nice suit, looked like a school principal who'd caught him doing something wrong.

What was the word for feeling embarrassed for someone else? Was there a word?

I needed to look it up.

Because I felt embarrassed for the Flee. But it didn't look like he cared how ridiculous he was acting, arms waving, mouth hollering so loud that the neighbors with the still-deflated snowman flipped on their porch light.

So I went to the living room to get reinforcements. I had to stand in front of the TV to block the stupid Military Channel show.

I put my arms out to show my annoyance.

"Remove your blockade," Grandpa shouted.

I wrote super fast: FRONT YARD THE FLEE WHAT ARE YOU GOING TO DO?

"Nothing. Not going to do anything. It's not my fight."

I wrote: MOM!!!!?????

Unfortunately for me, there is no volume control on what you write down on a piece of paper. I wish there were, but all you can do is add exclamation points, and that is also not very effective, because if you *really* know the origin of this symbol, you know that its fifteenth-century meaning was to show admiration or joy.

And I wasn't showing admiration or joy.

Grandpa said, "Listen, you want some advice? Here it is. Prepare to be amazed."

I prepared.

"Before you go taking the bull by the horns, make sure it's your bull," he said.

I can't even tell you what my expression was then, but I can tell you it compromised my left eyebrow growth.

I guess he read my confusion because he said, "Wayne, that means you figure out which fights are yours to fight. That bull out there is not ours. This is your mother's bull. Let her take it on. Besides, your mother must learn to take care of herself, because..." Grandpa trailed off. He left me hanging, wondering if he was about to share information. Information that I definitely didn't want to be a fact.

"Now, stop talking, Wayne, and enjoy this show."

News alert: I'd stopped talking weeks ago.

Still, I plopped down on the stupid flowery sofa and watched the military show on tank construction. But I didn't *enjoy* it. By the time a tank had its caterpillar tracks installed, we heard the front door slam, followed by the click of Mom's heels on the tile floor. Then she plopped down next to me and tossed the concert T-shirt onto my lap. The Bruh. He'd gone to the Bruh concert without me.

We all watched the next show about the history of camouflage.

I learned that the horned lizards of North America evolved ways to flatten their bodies to eliminate shadow.

After a little while, the doorbell rang. Why couldn't he stop messing with our lives? So I got up to answer the door.

"Leave it, Wayne," Mom said, but I brushed past her. Not that I had any idea what to say, because, you know, I was unable to actually *say* anything. Somehow, I was going to let him know that he could keep his stupid T-shirt.

I got to the door, and do you know what I saw?

Tim LeMoot with pizzas.

"Anybody order an Italian dinner?" he asked.

I guess I just stood there feeling stunned. Stupefied. Bewildered, even. I didn't let him in the door until he spoke again.

"I promised an Italian dinner and I intend to deliver, if that's okay with you, Wayne?"

So I let him inside and led him to the living room. Mom smiled. And she forgot to keep her head tilted to the right to cover up her missing eyebrow, too.

Tim LeMoot put the pizza boxes on the coffee table.

"Again, just wanted to say it was really nice to meet you, sir," the Boot said, and extended his hand toward Grandpa. Grandpa just gave him a nod. "Hope that little dustup in the front yard didn't ruin everyone's evening."

"Well, it's not your fault that old boy is, um, what's that saying?" he said, snapping his fingers. "Dumber than a..." Grandpa paused, trying to grab onto a word. But the Boot grabbed onto the silent space and ran with it.

"Dumber than a post, sir?"

The Boot actually said that. True story.

Grandpa raised an eyebrow. A thought was forming in his mind. "Dumber than a barrel of hair." He'd taken the Boot's bold statement as a challenge.

"Dumber than a wagon wheel?"

"That one's good." Grandpa stood up. "How about, so dumb he can't ride and chew at the same time?"

"If dumb was dirt, he'd cover about an acre." Man, I had to laugh at that one. The Boot was funny.

"He could fall up a tree."

"He's got a big hole in his screen door."

"He's got horns holding up his halo," Grandpa said.

Grandpa put his hands in his belt loops and squared off in front of the Boot. The Boot took off his suit jacket and rolled up his sleeves. Mom and I shared a look. Something I couldn't begin to name had just happened between Grandpa and the Boot, but it seemed like a good thing. Like something had been settled. Mom shrugged her shoulders and half smiled. This was bound to be more entertaining than any TV show about camouflage. In fact, the more we watched, the more I thought it *could* be a TV show: *Drill Sergeant vs. TV Lawyer. Tonight at ten!*

"If he was bacon, he wouldn't sizzle."

"He carries his brains in his back pocket."

"He's so crooked that if he swallowed a nail, it would come out a corkscrew."

Grandpa paused again. We waited for his next volley. "So, you're a lawyer, then."

"Where do you think I collected all those insults?" the Boot said. "Sir."

"Is that so?" Grandpa asked. "I collected mine training new recruits."

"Just yesterday, someone said that if a duck had my brains, it'd fly north for the winter," the Boot said with a smile. "I'm keeping that phrase for later."

"I could have used that one back in the day." Grandpa laughed. "Boy, Reed would have laughed at that phrase, yes, sir. He loved collecting those."

I froze. I watched and waited for Uncle Reed's ghost to flash in front of Grandpa. For a nanosecond, I saw it. Grandpa paused and remembered. His face looked pained. He twisted his mouth and he squinted his eyes. No one else saw it but me. I could tell he'd steadied himself by taking a deep breath and then clearing his throat. "Now, this pizza for all gathered here, then?"

He'd changed the topic.

"Yes, sir," Tim LeMoot said.

Everyone dug in. Except me. The pizza smelled delicious. My taste buds were in agony. Grandpa and Tim

LeMoot and Mom ate it all up. Sometimes I don't think they knew how they tortured me with their meals. I was forced to suck on a piece of crust like it was a baby's pacifier. All my *feelings* about pizza surfaced all over again.

True story.

When they all forgot I was in the room and began talking about places they'd like to travel, I snapped another stealth picture of the Texas Boot and sent it to Denny.

Boot eats pepperoni pizza!

I'd become a fan of the Boot. I admit it. In the hour I'd known him, he'd already kept a promise. He made my mother smile and not wear her *I need to watch English movies* face. And he even stood boot-to-boot with Grandpa.

It occurred to me that things might be looking up for Mom. We hadn't talked about the crash since New Year's Eve. We were getting distance from it. My face and throat were healing, and I was going to school. She'd just gotten her arm brace removed, was back at work, and was now going on dates! I was even beginning to wonder if Grandpa was going to move back to his house. I didn't really want to know, so I didn't ask.

Pretty soon, there wouldn't be any obvious evidence that we'd been in a plane crash. Except for a brand-new dishwasher and the blank space up on the Wall of Honor where the burial flag should have gone. A space that seemed to get larger. I mean, it just seemed like the land of AFTER was going on and on and on. And people could tell jokes in your living room and eat pizza. And no one was remembering BEFORE the way Grandpa did. The way he had memories of Uncle Reed that would stop him on a dime. I wondered if pretty soon anyone would remember that much of how it was before. When Uncle Reed was here. Before everything happened.

I went to my room, sat down on the floor of my closet, and opened the cardboard box that contained the display case for an American flag. Had it been a dumb idea to buy it? Sometimes I thought that was true. Sometimes I thought the case was my own personal elephant in my own room. I put the case on my carpet floor and touched the glass. It made me think back to Uncle Reed's funeral.

Did you know that Arlington National Cemetery is located on Confederate general Robert E. Lee's confiscated estate? The government seized the property in 1864 after a tax bill of $92.07 went unpaid. The first military man to be buried there was Private William Christman, a twenty-one-year-old private whose soldier's pay was only $13.41 per month. Soldiers from every single war in US history were now buried there. There were an estimated four hundred thousand graves at Arlington.

That day, it was four hundred thousand plus one.

Four enlisted men in uniform and white gloves lifted the American flag above Uncle Reed's coffin. They folded it over and over until it formed the shape of a triangle and the white stars were on top.

I'd looked it up.

I remembered sitting there at the cemetery and looking over at Grandpa, watching him keep it together. Watching him move his fingers behind his aviator sunglasses and wipe away a tear. I told myself I hadn't seen that. So I looked down, stared at my suit jacket, and focused on the buttons. Navy blue with gold on the edges.

They presented the folded honor flag to Grandpa. He passed it to Mom while he shook hands with soldiers who'd served with Reed. She placed the flag in her lap and reached for my hand and squeezed it. I remember praying she wouldn't look at me, either.

I understood something. Something I didn't really want to understand, but the realization forced itself into my brain uninvited. How tough had it been for Grandpa to bury his only son?

Pretty tough.

And then we'd almost died on the way home. What

if everyone had perished? Grandpa would have been left behind.

Mom knocked on my door. Quickly, I covered the empty flag case with bubble wrap.

"Can I come in?" she asked.

I opened the door, then sat down on my bed and picked at a loose string on my comforter.

"You know, maybe it wasn't very nice to make those jokes about your father."

Yes. There should be a rule. Only a family member can make fun of a family member.

"You probably have the idea that there's nothing good about him, Wayne. But he had some good qualities."

Yeah, like setting off explosives inside his house. Genius!

She sat down next to me and touched my hair the way moms do.

"Sometimes people aren't who you think they are at first. That's how it was for me and your dad. I had to speak up for myself. And for you. But he's maturing, I think."

You wouldn't think he was mature if you knew about that day he came over and hit me and Grandpa chased him off.

"Just be careful about expecting too much from him, okay?"

I turned my head away.

"The best thing he ever did was to give me you," she said. "What I'm trying to say is that even a flower can grow in the desert. You know, something beautiful can come from something...dry."

Dry?

"You know what I mean. Something good from an unexpected source."

I sort of understood what she meant about my dad. Even if she was comparing *me* to a flower and the Flee to an uninhabitable climate.

"Do you want to talk about it?"

No. I stared hard at the carpet on my floor.

Then she saw what I was looking at. The flag display case.

"Is that what I think it is?" she asked, her voice full of surprise. Hello, elephant in my room.

I've been looking for the flag.

She put her hands to her mouth. She was trying to hide her face. The sad face. We stared at the empty case.

Weeks ago, I'd told Denny that I was certain the flag would be found by the time the investigators announced the initial findings and cause of our crash. Why had I been so certain?

Why?

The report was due out on Monday.

DATA

NTSB initial report on Flight 56 released two months following the crash:

- *32 people died, including passengers and flight crew.*

- *Severe winds were a factor in the crash.*

- *During an earlier scheduled inspection, it was noted that there were fatigue cracks along the seam of the aircraft.*

- *The cracks had not been repaired.*

- *The fatigue cracks, coupled with wind shear, ripped open the hole in the plane.*

- *Therefore, a human error, or failure to adequately maintain the aircraft, was listed as the primary cause.*

CHAPTER 21

I expected weather to be the primary culprit of the crash. The storm. The winds. All of it pushing down our plane.

It was not. It was only listed as a factor.

So now I considered fatigue cracks. Tired spaces in the plane.

And it blew out and gave up during a freak December thunderstorm over East Texas.

It was a week after I'd first met Tim LeMoot. He and Mom were sitting at our kitchen table, drinking iced tea and checking movie times. I showed Mom the NTSB report I'd found on the Internet.

"It's difficult to accept."

Yeah.

"Do you feel better now that you know the facts?"

Sucks.

"I have to agree with you."

No amount of money will put the plane back together.

And Tim LeMoot chimed in. "Not that plane, Wayne. But others. Aircraft are designed by humans, and humans make errors. Sometimes you must hold people accountable."

Right.

"Hey, I have to go shoot a new commercial later. Want to go with us?" Tim LeMoot asked. It turned out that Tim LeMoot, in real life, was a nice guy who actually asked people what they wanted to do. And because I wasn't used to that, I shrugged and left them. They were happy. I could only pretend to be happy for so long.

I wasn't. I was too distracted. The NTSB report made everything about the crash final. Would that mean no more searches through East Texas? No more newscasts about the tragedy? I guessed the answer was no. There was already a sinking cruise ship off the coast of Italy eating up all the tragic news time, anyway.

Liz Delaney was probably researching that story right now.

Liz Delaney had not answered my *third* e-mail request. Denny had even left a message on her voice mail: "Hello,

Ms. Delaney, I hope it's not rainy. Respond to your e-mail from Mr. Kovok so he won't go into shock."

Liz Delaney probably thought she was being pranked. Denny used his whisper-voice, which could sometimes sound a little murdery over the phone.

Reporters were not responding to my e-mails.

And Sandy Showalter? I expected a report on the demise of our sort-of-boyfriend/girlfriend status any day now.

The primary cause of this relationship ending was a lack of interest.

But, the day before, Sandy Showalter had allowed me to walk all around the mall with her. And I mean from the Pizza Kitchen to Sears. End to end. The only thing we had in common was that we both avoided eye contact and sipped on drinks I bought when we passed the food court. Her mother had run off someplace in the mall to buy plates that were on sale.

I knew it was all pretend. As long as I was mute, I was her sort-of boyfriend. As soon as Dr. P pronounced me healed, Sandy's mother would allow her to bolt.

So I'd gathered up a bunch of facts and wrote a note to Sandy. I tried to be like old Wayne, giver of facts. Facts doing the talking so that I wouldn't sound stupid.

Want to know what it said?

Did you know that the word "muffin" is believed to come from the French term "moufflet," which means "soft bread"? And also, the corn muffin is the official state muffin of Massachusetts, and the apple muffin is the state muffin of New York?

"Ohhhhh," she said as she handed the note right back to me. The way she said it and carried out the word *oh* with three syllables had a lot in common with the way Anibal Gomez had given me the dog-dump glare and said *Duuuuude.*

Her look gently approximated the dog-dump glare.

My recitation of facts backfired.

Even for Wayne Kovok, it was a new low. It wasn't the ground floor of dorkery. No, there was a level beneath that. I'd ridden the elevator all the way to the basement of awkwardness.

I bet Sandy wrote a novel-length text to her friend Wendy about what a muffin-researching moron I was.

Now I sat on my bed thinking about the previous day. And I got so sick of myself. So sick of thinking and wondering. I went back to the kitchen table, where Tim LeMoot and Mom were still drinking iced tea.

I'll go to your commercial shoot.

"That's great," Tim LeMoot said.

We spent the rest of the afternoon watching Tim

LeMoot stand in front of a green screen inside a studio. He'd shout his phone number into the camera, practically begging accident victims to call him. His production team superimposed fake explosions, shattered glass, a bald eagle, and a giant black boot in the background.

Then they brought out actors to stand in front of the screen and shout about their fake injuries and how much money Tim LeMoot had kicked into their pockets.

Then they put Tim LeMoot up high on a ladder.

"This is the part where the team will superimpose the giant eighteen-wheeler," Mom whispered to me.

The last scene. Tim LeMoot stood in front of the green screen, and then they superimposed a giant field of grass behind him. I didn't get it at first. Why a field?

Tim LeMoot looked directly into the camera and said, "WHY WERE *YOU* IN AN ACCIDENT? WELL, ACCIDENTS HAPPEN TO GOOD PEOPLE. GOOD PEOPLE NEED SOMEONE LOOKING OUT FOR THEM! YOU NEED A LAWYER WHO'S OUTSTANDING IN HIS FIELD. SO CALL ME, TIM LEMOOT, THE TEXAS BOOT. I'M OUT STANDING IN MY FIELD! WHY SHOULD YOU GO THROUGH HARD TIMES ALONE? WHY?"

At the end of that session, the entire crew clapped. The Boot took a bow. The field disappeared from the screen.

Do you know what I was thinking? That Tim LeMoot seemed to understand the plaguing question.

Why should any of us go through anything all alone?

It all made sense now. The real reason Grandpa had come to live with us. The real reason he was still here.

Why should anyone go through hard times—or an illness—alone?

CHAPTER 22

So I was going to talk to Grandpa as soon as the sun rose in the morning. I hoped he would point to the elephant in the room and say, *Yep, there he is and his name is Dave. And me and my elephant are here because we didn't want to be alone while I have stomach problems that may or may not be cancer.*

But I didn't get the chance, because Grandpa answered the phone, took a message, folded it into a paper airplane, and aimed it at my head, and then I had to go eat with the Flee.

Epic fail.

Epic.

Epic.

Epic.

Grandpa said, "It might be a good idea. Considering."

Considering what?

Some unspoken message passed between him and Mom that I couldn't decipher. I suspected it had something to do with all the elephants living in our house.

Because if Grandpa thought it was a good idea to go out with the Flee, the world had gone crooked.

"I'll go with you, Wayne," Mom said.

"Jennifer, let the boy handle it on his own," Grandpa said.

"I'm going with him," Mom said with a determination I hadn't heard in her voice since, well, since we lived in BEFORE.

I got inside Mom's car, not knowing what to expect and not really caring. Sandy had told me that the most epic poet of all time, old Bill Shakespeare, had once written that "expectation is the root of all heartache."

So I prepared to have zero expectations.

Like Mom told me.

Zero expectations = zero heartache.

Do you know where the Flee wanted us to meet him?

At a very international restaurant. The International House of Pancakes. Did you know that IHOP recently opened its first restaurant in the Middle East? It's true.

They opened one in Dubai. Maybe a lot of the world's problems could be solved over pancakes and boysenberry syrup, which is my favorite. Boysenberry syrup is a cross between four different kinds of berries (European raspberry, blackberry, American dewberry, and loganberry). Do not ask me why I know so much about this syrup. I just do.

"Something wrong with you?" the Flee asked.

No.

"Still can't talk yet, huh?" the Flee said, his mouth full of pancakes.

"His therapy is going great," Mom told him.

I knew he enjoyed how I couldn't talk. He probably liked me better this way.

I ordered a shake, and a sandwich I couldn't eat, but what the heck. He owed me at least a sandwich. While he stuffed pancakes into his mouth, the Flee managed to spit out a few words.

"Sorry about the other night," he said.

I studied the back of the ketchup bottle. One tablespoon has twenty calories.

"Sorry, Jennifer," the Flee said. "It's just your dad."

"You might want to stop talking now," she told him.

"Hey, here's something I thought Wayne might be interested in," he said, passing me a brochure. It was yel-

low, and on the front it read, JOIN THE AQUADUCKS THIS
SUMMER.

"I thought, you know, you might want to check out
the swim team at the rec center. If you aren't going to run
track and field, maybe this is the sport for you. What do
you think? I'll take you."

No.

"Well, why not? Don't you want to join something this
summer? Meet some new people?"

I shrugged.

"Think about it. It might be fun."

Sure.

I knew I wouldn't spend a minute thinking about his
stupid idea.

"Want to go shopping for your birthday next?"

I nodded.

"Great, I'm headed to the men's and we'll be on the
way. Anything you want!"

"You don't have to go," Mom said when he left.

She didn't have to say that. I wasn't going to go anywhere with him. I had a gut feeling the Flee was going to
ditch me.

When he left the table, I noticed a lot of happy families were eating at IHOP. When you want something in
your own life, it looks like everybody at every table in a

restaurant has it. I'm not just talking about eyebrows. All over IHOP, people were having a great time. So why couldn't we?

When the Flee came back, his ear was to his phone. Across the table, half of my DNA stuffed pancake into his mouth as he talked.

"Yeah, yeah, calm down. I'm having lunch with my number one son." He winked at me. "Fine, fine. Okay. Don't have a cow."

Yep, I'd seen it coming.

From what I gathered, Stephanie was having some kind of emergency that required his immediate attention. He paid with a coupon, made a big production out of telling the waitress it was my birthday and "customers eat free on their birthday," and then I wrote a note to the waitress asking for a to-go box for my uneaten sandwich. He threw a twenty-dollar bill at me and told me he'd call me later and we'd do that shopping trip.

Loserberry.

Mom and I drove home in silence. I went inside the house and put my sandwich away. I rearranged Mom's blue glass birds into a circle, like she liked them. Why couldn't people leave things the way other people liked them?

Next to the sink, there was an amber pill bottle. One I

hadn't seen before. It was a prescription made out to Truman Dalton.

Right then I knew I'd chicken out on asking Grandpa anything. I didn't know if I really wanted the answer.

I pushed the AquaDucks brochure in front of Mom's face.

"Well, I get it," she said. "He's trying to encourage you to do something."

Remember the last time he encouraged me to do a sport? We all remember how great that was.

"It's true that your father didn't handle that well," she said. "I can't believe I'm going to say this, but I think he's right to want you to try new things."

It all made me think of that time the Flee did what he did. So I stopped thinking.

Grandpa walked in. His timing was perfect.

"What the heck is an AquaDuck?" he asked.

Going out!

"Mashed potatoes for dinner!" Mom said, and I headed for the door.

I wandered down Cedar Drive by myself and into the smooth streets of the Estates, kicking the same acorn for two blocks. The sky changed into a mix-up of oranges and purples, and the clouds looked like controlled explosions.

Maybe I did know something about poetry after all.

Or maybe the sky was distracting me. It worked. It made me think about a new topic. Something I'd just read that I couldn't wait to share with Denny Rosenblatt.

The Irish crown jewels have been missing since 1907. The jewels had been transferred to a safe in 1903. The new safe was to be placed in a newly built vault, but the safe didn't fit through the doorway to the vault. So the safe was then stored in a heavily locked office. Four years later, the jewels were stolen from that office.

Office versus Vault. Talk about heartache.

Among my many questions that start with the plaguing word is this: *Why* didn't builders measure the new safe *before* building the doorway to the new vault?

DATA

Returned e-mails from Liz Delaney: zero

Questions I still have for Liz Delaney: one million

Internet hours spent reading her articles and online biography: four

Data collected: Liz Delaney's great-aunt perished more than sixty years ago in a plane crash just out-

side Marshall, Texas. The flight left Dallas and was bound for Shreveport, Louisiana. According to reports, on May 17, 1953, the airliner flew through a thunderstorm and plunged to the ground thirteen miles east of Marshall. There were twenty souls aboard the aircraft. There was only one survivor. Since then Liz Delaney has had a special interest in aircraft disasters.

CHAPTER 23

My head was dizzy and excited about finding the Liz Delaney information. It felt like a weird connection. We were both interested in doomed flights over East Texas. If she only knew our story, she could help! I was sure of it. So I fired off another e-mail to her and hoped for the best.

Next, I received a text from Dennis Alan Rosenblatt, a.k.a. Denny, who made tragic use of acronyms. And it completely took my mind off air disasters.

Do not 4get. My BM is at 10:30 on Sat.

Do you know why that is so hilarious? So hilarious that I fell off my bed laughing and Grandpa Grouch shouted through my closed door, "Keep it down in there, soldier!"

My new and improved post-crash laugh still sounded like a sick donkey.

Anyway, here is a truth: People will make fun of you if you use acronyms incorrectly. It has happened to me with disastrous consequences. Never text *anyone* you are having a BM, okay?

BM = bowel movement.

So I wrote back to Denny:

Wow, you know the exact time of your BM??? How long have you been timing them?

I hadn't found anything that funny since one of the special gymnasts at the West Academy wore her shirt backward and didn't even know it. But aside from that, it was Denny's bar mitzvah, and I was excited to go.

Me: I'm going?

Denny: Of course, Wayne on a plane. Don't you want to hear me stutter through my Torah portion?

Me: You'll be okay.

Denny: I may have an actual BM. Very nervous! But there will be girls from my synagogue and they love the dance portion, so there's that. Wear a tie.

I wore a tie.

Now, I want you to picture me with all my many flaws, scars, a poorly tied tie (I wasn't about to invite Grandpa into my room, so I Googled how to do it), and a superthin left eyebrow as I entered Temple Emanu-El the morning Dennis Rosenblatt was to become a bona fide man.

You won't believe it, but I didn't look too bad. When you are in a room where every man is wearing a suit and the same type of hat, you fit in.

Mom had dropped me off at the synagogue. I went in and they fitted me with the yarmulke and handed me a program.

I expected the synagogue to look serious, and it did. It was all warm orangey colors, especially the oak pews, and the lights were low, so it made you know something important was about to take place. Mrs. Rosenblatt waved me up and sat me right next to Denny's grandmother.

"You sit with Bubbie, Wayne, my sweet little gentile."

Bubbie smiled at me and patted my hand with her dry fingers. "You could be Jewish. Your profile suggests a tribal lineage."

I didn't know how to answer this or if it was a true compliment. I just smiled and let her pat my hand some more. I noticed she had three rings on one hand.

"Bubbie will tell you what is going to happen. The Torah will be passed from the grandfather to the father to the bar mitzvah, Dennis. This symbolizes the passing down of the obligation to study the Torah. Our Dennis will recite his portion, and he will ask for a blessing from the rabbi. When he gets this blessing, he will now be responsible for himself and for following the commandments. Do you understand?"

I nodded, which, of course, was all I could do. In fact, it was what Denny had told me to do.

Denny had told me that his mother would sit me next to Bubbie.

Just before the ceremony, I sent Denny a text.

Me: What should I do?

Denny: Just nod. I, Denny Rosenblatt, am her second-favorite topic in the world. So just let her talk about me.

Me: What is her first-favorite topic?

Denny: Anything about dietary fiber and her need for more.

"Denny is my sweet, sweet little mensch," Bubbie said, still patting my hand. I figured we were on safe footing now that she'd brought up her second-favorite topic. I planned to do a lot of nodding to encourage her to stay on this topic. My knowledge of fiber was limited.

So I sat in the synagogue pews and watched Denny

as he was surrounded by his grandfather and father and as the Torah scrolls, wrapped in blue velvet with golden trim, were passed from one man to the next. Denny's face told the whole story. He was ready to receive them. There was a part of the ceremony where the congregation answered in unison, and I had no idea what it meant or what they said. I just focused on the story of Denny's face, which was fixed in concentration as the Torah scrolls were unrolled on a table.

The rabbi took part of his shawl and touched the spot where Denny was to read. Denny took his own shawl, touched the spot on the parchment, and then kissed the edge of his shawl. He rolled the scrolls back together and they all prayed. When he placed a pointer on the scrolls, he began his Torah portion. The words came out of his mouth like a chant. Like he was almost singing. Bubbie leaned into my shoulder and wept. So I patted her hand.

I couldn't believe how the entire synagogue was transfixed by Denny Rosenblatt, the bar mitzvah of the day, the guy who sang most of his sentences in real life and followed beautiful girls at the mall. His voice, normally such an annoyance to his mother because of his stuttering, became something altogether different. Chill bumps rose from the back of my neck. He rang out in song-talk so beautifully that you just knew he was born to sing.

Afterward, his mother and father and grandfather could not stop kissing him and patting him on the back. Denny had the biggest smile in the world. It was amazing to see the actual moment when Denny the boy became Denny the man.

I admit that I had a case of Jew envy. It's possible I always will.

The whole weight of thousands of years of tradition between fathers and sons made me so happy for Denny.

"We'll go to the party now, okay? You'll have fun with Dennis, yes?" Bubbie asked.

We went to the party.

Three hours after he became a man, Denny Rosenblatt had a big party in a hotel ballroom. Giant platters of food, a DJ, all kinds of funny blinking-light sunglasses, and dancing. It was all great to me, but Denny just sat at a big round table, looking across the room.

What?

"Max Goldsticker is talking to Monica with his perfect voice."

I lined up my sight to see who Denny was looking at. A pretty curly-haired girl with big, dark eyes. Monica.

Do you want to go over there?

"What would I say?" Denny asked. "I stammer on the name Monica."

233

You could sing. That works.

Denny wasn't budging. The whole room was supposed to be a party. A celebration for him. But he was miserable. I had an idea and didn't know if I could pull it off. The only fact I had about my idea was that Denny *really* could sing.

My idea led me to the stage, where the band was about to start playing a new song. A Beatles song I'd written down on a piece of paper and handed to them. A song I'd heard Denny sing in his mom's van a hundred times. One of the band members picked up the microphone and announced to the crowd that the next number was going to come from the guest of honor. Denny looked at the stage and at me. He shook his head, but I waved him up. If I could stand up there in front of a bunch of strangers with my beat-up face, I knew he could do this. And he would be impressive.

It was shouts from the crowd that finally got Denny up onstage. I made to head down the stairs, but Denny caught me by my arm before I could bolt.

"No way are you leaving," he whispered. While Denny sang and the audience cheered, I stood in the background and watched him. Denny was as happy as I'd ever seen him. I spotted Monica in the crowd, and she was no longer talking to Max Goldsticker. She was singing along with Denny.

When it was over, Mrs. Rosenblatt hugged and kissed Denny. And Denny had a small group of people around him, too.

I sat at a table of Rosenblatts and they had twelve conversations going all at once and it was terrific. I pictured them all on the same plane, all on the same flight, just having one big party in the sky.

"Oh, Wayne, honey, look at your friend Dennis, isn't he handsome tonight, I'm all verklempt," Mrs. Rosenblatt said. "He has the voice of an angel, my Denny, doesn't he? Wayne, honey, when is your birthday?"

I smiled at her.

Did you know that I was also about to turn thirteen?

Yep. If I had Hebrew blood, I was on the verge of being a man. I could stand out in the Flee's front yard, and he could say, *Here, son, have my collection of concert T-shirts.*

"I'm going to make you a delicious sandwich for your birthday, Wayne," Mrs. Rosenblatt said.

"Moooom, no one wants a sandwich for his birthdaaay!" Denny sang.

CHAPTER 24

Apparently, Denny Rosenblatt thought he knew what I needed for my birthday. Because three weeks later, when I turned thirteen, I went to his house and he chucked a big book at me. *The Illustrated History and Mystery of the* Titanic.

The Titanic?

Denny whisper-talked, "It's a metaphor for your life, Wayne on a plane."

My life is sinking into a watery grave?

"No, your life is about holding out hope. Lost things being found and all that. For your search. It's still out there waiting to be found. See? Do you know how long it took for searchers to find the sunken *Titanic*?"

Over seventy years.

"Exactly! So you've only been searching for the flag a few months. You need to give yourself time. I was wrong about what I said before. You should keep looking."

It was a nice thought. That Denny. He could not only sing, he could really surprise you with the connections he made in his brain. But the thing was, I didn't really think I had a lot of time.

Grandpa was thinner. Sleepier. Another new amber pill bottle was on the counter. Facts were adding up. And I still hadn't come right out and asked him what was up. I drew pictures of elephants and pinned them to the fridge. The computer's screen saver was a giant elephant. I was hoping he would ask me, *Hey, what's up with all these elephants?* And it would be a good place for me to respond, *It's about time we talk about all these elephants in the room, huh?*

It hadn't worked.

And Mom? She was a locked door. She was in a good mood when she was with Tim LeMoot. But when she was at home, alone and quiet, her mood seemed sad. She wore her deep-thinking face all the time. The face you have when you are trying to work out a really hard word problem.

Sandy? Well, the *Titanic* metaphor fit our relationship better than any other. Our steady stream of back-and-forth texts had continued, if you could even call them texts. We were down to communicating only in emojis.

So the flag? I didn't have seventy years. Though there was still no new news, I held out hope that a stranger would discover it. I imagined it in my head every night. Maybe if I imagined it enough, it would come true.

"Come on, let's go walk around Sears," Denny said.

We got to the mall, and Denny said now that we were thirteen, we should wear cologne.

"We'll walk through Macy's. Those fragrance women in white coats? Man, they spray everything that moves," he whispered.

He was right about that. We walked right into the cologne gauntlet. At least three white-coated women with press-on smiles were armed with cologne bottles and ready to shoot.

I got one cologne attack. Denny got three. As I walked behind him into the mall, the wake of smells that trailed him was toxic. But he thought he smelled like a man. There was no arguing with him about that.

"Girls love cologne," Denny whispered.

When you don't have a properly working voice, you let a lot of things go. Like the effectiveness of too much cologne. So I shook it off, and then he said we should make up a story to go along with my look.

I don't have a look.

"You might have been in a motorcycle accident, you know? Or you are a young movie stuntman on hiatus. You're here to get a jacket, right?" Denny whispered. "Let's go to Leather Town. I've always wanted to go in there."

True. Mom had told me to buy a new jacket since I'd outgrown my old one.

You know how something leathery and new smells extra-leathery? That's what the jacket I found smelled like. Soft as butter, too. I didn't look half bad when I turned to the mirror and checked out my right-side profile. Man, I wouldn't be half bad if I could go through life walking sideways.

I wrote to Denny: Cool.

After our trip to the mall, you will never guess what was waiting for me when I got home!

"Surprise," Mom shouted. "Happy birthday!"

Mom had pulled every chair we owned around our kitchen table.

And Sandy Showalter was seated in one of them.

Sandy Showalter in my house! There were other

people, too, but it was like they were in black and white and she was in full color. I would like to tell you that this fact made me super happy. And it would have if Sandy hadn't been sitting in a green-and-white lawn chair. Her mother sat in a lawn chair, too. The Flee, Stephanie, and Carrot sat in our regular chairs. Grandpa was in the swiveling office chair. Mrs. Rosenblatt sat in the tiny antique chair Mom kept in her bedroom. Because we didn't have enough regular chairs. I tried not to focus on that fact. Mismatched chairs should not make a person feel embarrassed, but they did.

"Wayne, you and Denny sit right here," Mom said.

We sat on two stools. I don't even know where they came from.

Stupid chairs.

Did you know that there are several recorded cases of spontaneous human combustion? The common denominator, however, is that most of these people drank alcohol to excess prior to their combustion. The best I could've hoped for in my fantasy combustion was that I'd been spritzed with cologne to excess.

Because cologne is also highly flammable.

"Happy birthday, Wayne," Sandy said with a smile.

A real, in-person smile, not an emoji smile! "I like your jacket."

So I didn't go up in flames, unless you counted the hot rash that crept up from my stomach to my neck.

Denny sang, "There will be caaaaakkkkke!"

Our stools were right on the corner of the table. No easy exit. And believe me, since the crash, I pay attention to the exits in a whole new way.

Mom put a supersized bowl of ice cream in front of me, while everyone else gobbled up delicious-looking, torturous pizza. Even Grandpa. Everyone was talking and smiling, even Sandy. I realized that Mom was happy. Her hair up in a ponytail. Her new eyebrow debuting.

"Tim is coming over later, Wayne," she said, smiling. "He has something for you, too."

"What? Probably a pair of boots, right?" the Flee said.

I saw Mom mouth the word *behave* to him. I hoped he would, but my stomach did flip-flops. Maybe the worst thing he would do was tell me to join the stupid Aqua-Duck team in front of everyone.

"I would never miss my son's birthday," he said. Carrot and Stephanie had ice cream.

"Daddy got you money," Carrot blurted out.

"Carrot, son, you shouldn't spoil it," the Flee said.

Denny sang-talked. Mrs. Rosenblatt rambled on about Denny's bar mitzvah and how the printer had messed up the spelling of his name on the thank-you cards and called him Danny. Even old Hank Williams, whose tank was in the room, took a slow swim around his habitat. And it wasn't awkward silence with Sandy.

"Everyone misses you at school," Sandy said.

I wrote her a note: *Thanks!*

Grandpa handed my dad a piece of cake.

"Well, age thirteen, huh," Grandpa said. "That's a great age. When Reed was thirteen, do you remember, Jennifer, he was already working his way up to be an Eagle Scout. He organized an event to help the local animal shelter and did it all himself. That boy already knew how to serve his community and his country."

Grandpa entered the patriotic zone. That wasn't so bad. He was most like himself when he did that. Not sad or distracted. I hoped the conversation about Reed wouldn't get him all worked up.

I looked at Denny and envied him all over again. His dinner table was always loud, but there wasn't any sadness. And bonus fact: All his dining room chairs matched.

So I prayed hard that everyone would stay happy. Just one hour of solid happiness. Just one hour where it could be all about me. Maybe that sounds selfish, but that was what I wanted. Eat cake. Be happy. Receive presents.

Mom put a box in front of me. A new laptop computer. Finally! Mrs. Rosenblatt gave me an engraved silver money clip with my initials. W.H.K.

And Grandpa? He presented me with a new fishing pole. Man, the whole party was *almost* nice.

And it was all going well. Until Grandpa asked the Flee a question.

"So, Doug, where do your people come from again?" Grandpa asked.

"My people?" the Flee said. "You make it sound like I'm from another planet or something." He laughed and it made Mrs. Rosenblatt laugh, too.

"Your people. Any of them serve?" Grandpa continued.

"Now, Stephanie, this is the thing I told you about," the Flee said. "It was always about the army in this family. Who served. Who fought the longest."

"What's wrong with the army?" Grandpa asked.

"It's fine. It's just not for everyone. And you already know the answer to your question. None of my people served." He put the word *people* in air quotes.

It was possible, I thought, that the Flee felt like me

sometimes. Like he didn't fit in. Like he was the odd lawn chair around a table of matching chairs. I took a bite of ice cream and looked at Denny. He gave me a nod and a smile.

"Does anyone want any more cake?" Mom offered.

"I guess some families get to sit back and stay at home while their liberties are being protected by others," Grandpa said. "Wayne, you understand that, right? When you enlist, you'll see how exceptional it is to serve."

"What if Wayne doesn't want to enlist?" the Flee said.

There it was again. A play called *Tug-of-War*. Wayne Kovok playing the role of the rope. Stretching. Pulling. I prayed Grandpa would drop the subject. Embrace his own rule about knowing when it's your bull. This wasn't his bull. But that didn't stop him from waving a bright red cape and trying to agitate my dad for sport.

In front of everyone.

"It's less about choosing to enlist and more of a calling," Grandpa said. "Wayne will make the right decision."

Wait, what? What is the right decision? And why was this conversation taking place around the table? On my birthday?

Mom said, "Dad, you want some more ice cream?" Maybe she thought if people were stuffing themselves with ice cream, they couldn't talk. It was a good strategy.

"I don't know, Jennifer," the Flee said. "Do you have red, white, and blue flavor?" He tried to make a joke. Is it still a joke if no one laughs?

Grandpa ignored Mom. "You're good at running, though."

The Flee puffed up. "Well, I got a college scholarship for running track. Some people say I had a real talent for running."

"Well, don't break your arm patting yourself on the back," Grandpa said, which I thought was a little funny.

"Funny," the Flee said. "I was a champion runner."

"Ha! Running away, maybe," Grandpa said.

I stared into my bowl of ice cream. *Did you know that the biggest ice-cream sundae ever created weighed twenty-four tons?*

"Listen, I was teaching Wayne valuable life lessons. Endurance and such."

The most popular flavor of ice cream is vanilla.

"Okay, since I know the old man isn't going to drop it, what I did was take Wayne out to this road. To train him," the Flee said to everyone.

Ice-cream cones were invented in 1904 at the World's Fair in St. Louis.

"Doug, no one wants to hear about that," Mom said.

In my mind, I covered everyone with the twenty-four-ton ice-cream sundae. Except Sandy and Denny and Mom. I let them sit on imaginary ice-cream cones.

Grandpa interrupted. "You know what, Doug?"

"What?" the Flee asked.

"You're all beans and no broth!"

I stirred my ice cream until it was like soup.

"Doug! Dad! Let's change the subject," Mom said.

"Well, it's true!" Grandpa said.

If you thought that would make me want to shout at the top of my lungs, you'd be correct. And inside, I was. I was shouting. Thousands of shouts, pounding against the inside of my brain. I was desperate to shout. To shout, but my beat-up throat would not cooperate. My voice had progressed to a raspy whisper in Dr. P's office. Fact: A raspy whisper will not get anyone's attention.

"He was fine. Ask his mother. He was fine, right, Jennifer? He coulda been a track star if you'd let me keep training him."

"Training, huh?" Grandpa said.

I pictured my voice as a solid object trapped in a jar. If only I could smash the glass and let it go free. "You don't understand, do you?" Grandpa said. "Maybe you never will."

It was too much. I had to break the glass.

246

"New topic!" I said, jumping up from the table. I pounded the table with my palm. *Bam!* Mom flinched. Blinked. The sound had been louder than a raspy whisper.

Denny slapped his hand on the table, too. *Bam!* "Y-y-yeah. New topic!"

I stood up and then Denny did, too. Everyone looked at us like we'd just come from Mars.

Then Carrot slammed his hand on the table, too. "Yeah!" he said.

Long seconds passed before I walked out of the room. And Denny walked out with me. I went out the garage and down the alley and bolted.

CHAPTER 25

And Denny ran after me.

"Wayne...Wayne on a plane," Denny sang.

I waited for Denny to catch up. We stood in the middle of Cedar Drive. The stars were on fire like they were burning with anger. Like me.

"Wayne? Do you know what you just did? You spoke! You talked!" Denny sang.

"I know."

We walked all over the neighborhood. Past the water tower that went right on shining its red light as if nothing ever changed. Past the house that still had the stupid old flattened inflatable snowman in the front yard like they didn't know it was late February and whole seasons had changed and things were starting to turn green.

Hello, people! Be useful!

Past the houses in the Estates that had smooth streets no one skated on but me.

The cold air made my throat hurt, but we walked and walked until we got to the park and climbed up into the hard plastic rocket ship.

I hadn't spoken whole sentences for weeks, and now that I could, I pushed through the sandpapery soreness.

Dr. P would scold me later.

But sometimes you just have to get it out. I wanted to get everything out that night.

This is what I told Denny.

I was eight.

Mom and the Flee were married. We didn't have Mr. Darcy. The photos for the future Wall of Honor were all in a dusty album. But there was a shelf.

His shelf.

His stupid shelf.

It had ribbons and trophies for track and field.

I admired the shiny gold trophies and the blue ribbons that sent him to college. I wanted to be like him. I wanted to run fast. I wanted him to think I was like him. Maybe he'd like me. Notice me.

One day he said, *How 'bout we teach you some man skills?* And I was all up for it.

He drove us out into the country. Old gray roads near old yellow fields. That was what it looked like to me. Just roads and fields and sun and dust. No houses or street-lights, just a long hot road. So endless, it blended right into the horizon.

He stopped the car and told me to get out. And I did. I did whatever he said. He told me to stand at the back of the car and I did. Then he shouted, *Now run, boy!*

His car sped off and I ran after it. He slammed on the brakes as I caught up. Then he took off again. Same thing. Sprint. Stop. Sprint. Stop.

He hung out the window and shouted for me to run again, then he took off. He didn't stop. I ran and ran into clouds of dust and sun. I ran until I saw his car turn and disappear around a corner. I ran until my mouth was hot and dry.

Red taillights.

That was all I saw until I didn't see them any longer. They'd shrunk in the distance. Disappeared, leaving me lost in the dusty nowhere.

There are lots of words for *scared.* I experienced all of them at once. I thought, *Well, I'm going to die and I have to go to the bathroom and will I ever see Mom again?* Tears rose up as I ran down the road in the direction of the car. I ran and ran, and the tears didn't have time to fall. They dried on my face. And I remember thinking, if I could outrun the speed of tears, I'd be as fast as my dad. And then I didn't care if I did cry, because, you know, I was going to be dead soon, or worse. So I just sat beside the road and waited to die. I was sure I was going to die. Worse, I'd let my dad down.

Later, he zipped back down the road and shouted from the car window, *What a crybaby! I was just messing with you.*

And he did the whole thing again. Said he was going to do it until I stopped crying. Said he was thinking of just leaving me out there. I was ashamed. I'd let him down. Again.

Mom found out because I'd peed my pants while I was scared and alone. The rest of that night they argued.

Mom came into my room that night. She thought I was sleeping. She touched my head the way moms can't help but do and whispered, *I won't let that happen again. Ever.*

I hated running after that. I hated the shelf. I tried not to hate the Flee. He was my father, after all. So I distracted myself with books. When he tried to get me to do something with him, I hid in my room and read. The more facts I learned, the more he called me stupid. Which was stupid.

True story.

That was what I told Denny. My throat felt like a cheese grater had gone over it, but I'd said everything. My throat hurt, but my insides felt light.

"Grade A jerk," Denny said.

"You know what I hate? I hate that he just won't act like a grown-up. He didn't when I was a little kid and he still doesn't. Do you know he set off fireworks *inside* his house?"

"You feel better now?" Denny asked.

"I never told anyone that."

"You know what my Bubbie says about secrets?"

"What?"

"They are like farts. They have to bubble up eventually."

"Your grandmother didn't say that!"

"But it's still true, right? You feel relief after you get rid of both of them."

"True."

Walking back to my house that night, I looked at the sky. And even though I hadn't thought about God or praying very much, I said a silent prayer. It was simple. I asked God for courage to say things out loud.

Although, I admit, it scared me that God might give me what I asked for. What then?

CHAPTER 26

When I'd gotten back to the house with Denny, everyone was gone except Mrs. Rosenblatt. Mom and Grandpa were in the kitchen, cleaning up.

"I'm sorry," Mom said. Denny left and I went to my room. I wasn't going to tell her she didn't have to apologize. But it was really Grandpa's fault, anyway. He kept poking the Flee. He ruined my birthday. Let him be sorry.

Two days after that, Grandpa drove me to see Dr. P after school.

"You can talk now," Grandpa said. "Nothing to say?"

Nope.

Maybe I was being rude. Maybe I was a little mean. But I was still mad. He didn't have to go off like that at my birthday dinner. He could have done it when Sandy wasn't around, and I wouldn't have minded it one bit.

And then I was in Dr. P's office.

"So, Wayne, you can talk now?" Dr. Pajaczkowski asked. "And you can say my name out loud? Let's hear it."

"Sir, I'm not sure I could have said your name before my throat injury."

He laughed. "Fair enough. You can call me Fred."

"Thanks, Fred."

When we got home, I sat outside on the porch and waited for Sandy. I'd asked her to stop by after she got out of school. It seemed better to speak to her face-to-face. I'd made the decision to just rip the Band-Aid right off. Get it over with. Break up before she could do it to me. Because I understood something about girls and Sandy. I knew I liked having Sandy as a friend because she was always nice to me. Always. Why not try to stay friends so that it wouldn't be so awkward?

I had a book to read, but it sat there unread for a long time. Then I nearly pruned our front bush to death, picking all the crunchy leaves from it, tearing them in half, and tossing them to the sidewalk.

All these thoughts flew around my head and I wanted them to stop. So I dove into the book. You would think I'm a nut, but I was reading a book authored by a pilot that tells you everything you wish you could ask someone in aviation. If you were thirteen and had no access to a pilot in real life, this was the book for you.

According to Mom, anyway. She gave it to me for my birthday.

Anyway, I opened the book right at the chapter about bird strikes and planes. Bird strikes against airplanes are serious business, especially where the birds are concerned. Did you know some airports use border collies to keep the bird population down around the runways? Also, planes fly at two hundred fifty knots when they are at an altitude under ten thousand feet. This is supposed to minimize the damage caused by birds flying into engines.

But the thing is, why don't the stupid birds change course? Why aren't they scared away by the noise of the aircraft? Why can't they feel the change in the air?

Why?

Reading about this didn't take my mind off what I was about to do that afternoon.

I recognized her mom's muffin-delivering green car when it pulled up. Sandy got out of the car and walked up our cracked sidewalk. She held a muffin basket tight.

"Hi, Wayne," Sandy's mother shouted from the car. "Be back in a little bit."

"Hi, Wayne," Sandy said.

"*Cómo estás?*" I asked.

Sandy sat down next to me on the cold porch. I plucked more leaves off the bush and twisted and tore them into little pieces. "So, your voice?"

"Yeah. It's back," I managed to say in a scratchy tone. My new voice was deeper and different. Like it was the voice of someone else coming from inside me.

"That's so great." Sandy plucked the leaves from the bush on her side of the porch. "Are you going to come back to Beatty?"

"Probably. Probably next year."

"That's good."

Don't chicken out. Don't chicken out. You know what to do.

"Listen," I said.

For a second, I couldn't push any more words out of my mouth. I was too afraid. Why is the right thing to do often the hardest thing to do?

So I said, "We should still be friends, but I don't think we should sort of go out anymore."

Even though it made me more than a little sad to say these words to the most beautiful girl in seventh grade, all the awkwardness I'd felt around her decreased.

Sandy's response was quick as a wink.

"Okay," she said.

It was so fast it hurt a little. But she threw her arms around me in a hug, which knocked me halfway into the bushes. "Wayne, you're so easy to talk to. You're the best ex-boyfriend ever!"

"Feel free to spread that rumor around school," I said.

And then, as if it had all been a perfectly written scene in a movie, Mrs. Showalter hit the brakes in front of our house, Sandy bounced down the sidewalk, and their green car sped away from the scene of a breakup.

I looked at the front porch step.

There were two matching bald spots on the bushes flanking the sidewalk.

Well, I'd said what I needed to say.

After a while, a plane flew overhead pretty low. It wasn't a commercial jet but some kind of single-engine plane. I could tell by the sound. White wings with red tips at the ends. Not big enough to have a 14A. Probably only two souls on board. I lifted my hand to its underbelly and held it in the air until it was out of sight. It circled back around. A rising trail of smoke formed. Was the plane in trouble?

Mayday?

It went straight up and down and made one thick line in the air. I stood up to get a better look. The smoke stopped, turned on again, and formed the shape of a heart. Then it made a giant U.

I ♡ U.

The message hung in the air like white cotton suspended in blue sky.

A skywriter. Someone's message in the sky. A love message right at the moment I said good-bye to Sandy Showalter.

True story.

Sad story.

I waited for the skywriting to go all smudgy before I went inside. I went to the fridge and searched for something to eat. Using my voice to do the right thing had made me hungry.

Grandpa strolled into the kitchen.

"Win some, lose some, Wayne. It's tough to get dumped, isn't it?"

"I didn't get dumped. I was technically the *dumper*."

"Either way, the sound of heartbreak is loud and profound." I wished I still had my legitimate, plane crash–caused ability to *grrrr*. I would have *grrrrr*'d at Grandpa.

"Whatever." I opened the fridge and grabbed the milk.

"I guess your birthday could have been better if all that hadn't happened the other night," he said.

He arranged the blue glass birds on the counter into two straight and perfect rows, then turned and looked me square in the eye.

I knew what he was doing. That was how a drill sergeant said he was sorry. I wanted to say it was okay. But my awful birthday was like a bruise. The hurt spot would fade gradually, not right when you wanted it to. So I didn't say anything.

"Know what I think, Wayne?"

"No, sir."

"I think we need a cheeseburger. You can eat a cheeseburger now that you can talk again, right?"

We went out for a cheeseburger. Sure, I thought about being brave enough to come right out and set things square with Grandpa.

So, would you like a side of fries and to tell me what those pill bottles on the counter are for?

Yeah, I thought about it a lot. But, surprise, I had more thoughts than I could speak.

We sat in a booth at a restaurant, and the bubbly waitress with twelve thousand buttons on her shirt told us the day's special like a rapid-fire cheerleader drill.

"Okay, today's special is two entrees, one appetizer, two iced teas, and Death by Chocolate, all for one low price!"

"We'll take it!" Grandpa said.

Later, as we were starting dessert, Grandpa told me, "Don't give up, Wayne." And I wondered for the millionth time if Grandpa had mind-reading abilities. If maybe he'd looked behind my closet door and seen my dumb collection of facts that were leading me nowhere.

"Don't give up on what?"

"Girls. You'll find the right lid to your pot," he said, forking a big piece of cake. "She'll be in the least likely place. I met the love of my life at a hardware store."

"Did she look miserable?" I asked, thinking of Denny's theory of miserable girls.

"More like out of place. But that's why I noticed her." Grandpa looked across the restaurant, a sad expression on his face. "Your grandmother. She was special."

"Hey, did you know that the smell of chocolate increases theta brain waves, which induce relaxation?" I said. "Chocolate is also thought to increase blood flow to the brain, so it's possible that it makes you smarter."

"Well, look who's back, Mr. Fact." Grandpa grinned. "Let's order a second dessert!"

"Are you allowed to?" I asked.

Grandpa tilted his head to the side and gave me a look. I could have asked more questions. I could have tried to get information. I could have.

"I mean, I'm too full for any more dessert," I lied. "This is the most I've eaten in months."

CHAPTER 27

Three weeks and more phone calls to Liz Delaney later, and nothing had changed except muffins hardening on the kitchen counter. I don't know why I hadn't thrown them out.

I went to the West Academy and did my time there. The trio of gymnasts had gotten wise to my nerdiness and even asked for my help on a math project. I went to Dr. P for one last appointment. I read books. I read my collection of facts about the flag search. I read Denny's book about the *Titanic*. I read about a man who punched a two-hundred-pound alligator that had clamped onto his son's arm.

I did everything but actually use my voice. I'd always known I could be strange, but my silence surprised even me.

I brought our chess set into Mom's room.

"Want to play?" I asked.

She smiled, so I went in and set everything up on top of her comforter. Elizabeth Bennet from *Pride and Prejudice* was on the TV, and Mom muted the sound while we played.

"Tim LeMoot called," I told her.

"Do you like him?"

"He's okay," I said. "Maybe he's your Mr. Darcy."

"What do you know of Mr. Darcy?"

"You're kidding, right? You forced me to watch all that stuff. Plus, the dog."

"Forced you?"

I stood up and did my best high-pitched-voice interpretation of a young English woman having a cow about some guy. "Oh my, oh my, I'm in such a state because I need a husband. I think I'll go run across this field in the rain!"

"Wayne Howard!"

I turned my voice up a notch. "Oooh, ooooh, maybe the strong-booted Mr. LeMoot is in want of a good woman."

"Stop it!" She tossed a pillow at my face. My face didn't hurt anymore.

I pointed at the muted TV screen. "Look! She's running across the field in the rain! I told you."

After I took a bow for my performance, my audience of one was weeping. Not happy tears for my wonderful and moving portrayal of an English woman. But big, giant, sloppy tears.

"Mom?" I sat on the bed. "Hey, did you know that it was the Roman soldiers who first wore neckties? Then other armies wore them to signify their country's colors. And much later, the French used ties as a fashion statement, but they were meant to just absorb sweat, so it's sort of gross when you think about it."

Mom took me by the hands and said, "I love your brain. It's very handsome." Then she tried to touch my eyebrow, and because she was feeling bad, I let her do her mom thing.

"Did you know that the Jewish religion has six hundred and thirteen commandments to follow, as opposed to Christianity's ten?"

"Your scar looks better. You learned a lot from Denny."

"I guess."

"I missed hearing your voice."

My new voice still surprised me. Mom never said if it surprised her, too.

"Now, Wayne, listen. I have to tell you something.

About your grandfather," she said. She couldn't get the sentences out. She stuttered like Denny. I'd never seen her that rattled in my life, and that includes the month before we fled from the Flee.

"You don't have to say anything," I said. Now that Mom was going to come out and tell me, I didn't want to hear it. Because of what a jerk I was. I didn't think about how it was hurting her feelings, too.

"No, I need to. I need to tell you, but I don't know how to give you more bad news."

"What she's trying to say is that I'm dying. Ta-da!" There was Grandpa, standing in the doorway.

"Dad! I was trying to say it gently."

"You were saying it too slow," Grandpa said. "The truth doesn't take a lot of words. Sorry you had to find out this way, kid. You probably want to go eat a muffin now." He was smiling, teasing me. But it didn't feel right.

I waited to feel something. Something like relief. I waited for the mighty elephant to walk out of the room. But here's what they don't tell you about that phrase. When you *do* point to the elephant in the room and it finally disappears, it leaves a mighty space behind. A space so big that there's nothing else. My throat closed up. My heart sank.

Stupid elephant.

Because to tell you the truth, I'd imagined this day already. I'd say something to Grandpa like *I've known for a long time*, and then he'd say, *You're not as stupid as you look, Kovok*, and Mom would say, *Cut it out, you two.*

But none of what I'd imagined happened.

I didn't say anything. No one said anything.

Not a word. It was one of those long, stupid, agonizing, awkward silences that I hated with the intensity of a hot, red August sunburn.

Hate. Hate. Hate.

"Don't you have any questions?" Grandpa finally asked. He pulled a piece of paper from his pocket. "I even made a list of answers. I wanted to be prepared for your torrent of questions."

"Answers? Answers to what?"

"Well, for example, question one might be"—Grandpa began reading from his paper—"*How bad is it? Can't you have surgery?* and the answer to that is no, the cancer has spread to the liver."

I guess my throat told my feet to just run. Because that was what I did. I grabbed the piece of paper from his hand as I darted past him.

And I took off and was glad I'd been wearing my Adidas. I didn't take my phone, house keys, or anything. I went outside and jogged down Cedar, zigging and zagging all through the tree-named streets in the dark. It was a beautiful March night. Cool and moonlit.

I could tell it was the Car pulling up behind me. Just the sound of it purred like no other car on the road. But I kept running.

"How long are you going to jog?" Grandpa shouted. He'd put the soft top down on the convertible.

"Until I get tired," I said.

"I'm tired just watching you."

"Then go home!"

"Your mother is worried."

Tell me something I don't know.

"Hey, nice night to go to a drive-in for a shake. I'm buying!"

I stopped and looked at him. He idled the car. "Getting a shake doesn't solve everything," I said.

"We can talk about this, you know, Wayne. I know it's hard on you now that you just found out, but—"

"I've known for a while."

Grandpa smiled and turned his head at me. "Well, you're not as stupid as I thought, Kovok."

I got inside the Car.

New topic.

We went to Sonic and ordered thick, creamy milk shakes. Then we drove all over town with the radio turned up and the top down and looked at the constellations and the full moon.

"I taught Reed to drive in this car, you know."

Nope, didn't know that.

"I love how this car growls," I said.

"Son, Japanese muscle cars growl. *American* muscle cars *rumble*."

"Okay, I like how it *rumbles*!"

I don't know how long we drove, but it was long enough to finish our shakes and drive back to Sonic and get fries.

There wasn't a better distraction in the world.

True story.

CHAPTER 28

Good distractions, like driving classic cars in the moonlight, can't last forever.

It had been two long weeks since Grandpa and Mom told me the bad news. I'd tried hard to not think about him being sick. I stayed in my room and read. I watched every action movie I could find. I did all I could to not have to think about real life.

But real life creeps back in.

It creeps in right on a Friday night when you notice a forgotten piece of paper there on your desk, written in your grandpa's handwriting, with a list of answers, all bullet-pointed, neat, and full of data about terminal, untreatable pancreatic cancer. Data that told me he had been diagnosed months before Uncle Reed deployed (he didn't tell him), and how he kept eating cheeseburgers (when his doctor told him not to), and that his prognosis was three to six months (the average life expectancy after diagnosis with metastatic disease is just three to six months), but that the doctor said every patient's cancer is different, some live longer than others (*and I expect to, so don't worry, I'm not dying tomorrow*).

It was all right there. All the questions he knew I'd have. Because he knew me. He knew how my brain worked. It wanted the facts.

Stupid cancer.

Stupid.

Stupid.

Stupid.

I punched my wall. I punched it again. And again. Then I looked out my stupid window.

Did you know that it takes four hundred and fifty years for your average plastic water bottle to fully degrade? Plastic bags take ten to twenty years to degrade if exposed to air and sun, but five hundred or more years if they're dumped in a landfill. The reason is that microorganisms are put in landfills to eat the trash like food. No microorganism we now have recognizes polyethylene as food, and that's the main ingredient in a lot of plastics.

If my stupid neighbors thought that awful, old, flattened

plastic Christmas snowman was just going to automatically biodegrade and they wouldn't have to put it away, they were ignorant of the facts. Couldn't they see the lump-of-white-plastic ghost of Christmas past? Couldn't they see the obvious right in front of them?

Right in front of them!

So I did what I had to do. And I'm not sorry. No, I'm not sorry for what I did to that irritating hunk of nonbiodegradable stupid snowman that everyone up and down Cedar Drive *still* had to look at every stupid day. I mean, if he was still going to be there, either put it out of its misery or put it back to its original state.

Make it useful.

I crept over to my neighbors' yard and did a snatch-and-grab. I got the old snowman into my garage and inspected him. The tiny generator was still attached. My neighbors had just left the thing unplugged all this time. The snowman was chewed in a couple of places, probably by feral squirrels. There were a few surface tears in the plastic, but otherwise, he was still in one piece. I put duct tape over the tears so that he wouldn't leak. I got an extension cord, plugged him in, and waited for inflation. He popped like a giant kernel of popcorn. And there he was, staring at me with his Christmas grin, all happy and festive and thinking everything was still merry. Man, that made me mad. So I punched the snowman in the face. But that didn't do it. He still looked happy.

I reasoned that when I returned it, my neighbors would look like lazy spring morons with an outdated lawn ornament waving at the street. But as I stared at the dirty, chewed-up snowman, it occurred to me that he needed something extra to get the message across.

Using dark black markers, I made the snowman's eyes twice as big and connected his eyebrows. With a red marker, I drew a blood line down his mouth, and Snow Zombie was born!

I unplugged the extension cord, grabbed rolls of duct tape, and headed out of the garage. The zombie snowman rode on my skateboard down the back alley. The snowman lost a little air, but not too much. By the time I got to my neighbors' front lawn, I spotted the car. I didn't recognize him until it was too late.

Tim LeMoot, the Texas Boot. Tim LeMoot slowed down his car, looked me right in the eyes, and kept driving.

I quickly rigged Snow Zombie right up to the front door of my neighbors' house. I found the electrical outlet by the door, plugged him in, and waited for him to inflate face-first into their doorway, so that the first thing they'd see the next morning was a zombie snowman. *Take that, neighbors.*

Then I hotfooted it out of there. Lightweight. Like at least one thing was right in the world. One stupid snowman wasn't lying flattened but instead was doing what he was meant to do. Being who he was meant to be. For about two minutes, I felt useful. For about two minutes, I forgot about the list of answers.

Two minutes.

Then, out of nowhere, Mrs. Rosenblatt's van rolled up to the curb. And out popped Denny. And he walked up my walk, holding a pie with at least five inches of white meringue, and I was thinking I must have been having a weird dream. Because why would Denny show up on a Friday night with a pie?

The snowman. Denny. It was all just a dream.

Bam! Do you want to know what a pie to the face feels like? Because I can now tell you. I'm not just a crash survivor. I'm a pie-in-the-face recipient, too. A pie in the face will snap you into reality pretty quickly.

"You said you were my friend," he sang in a high-pitched song. And I felt sorry for him because I know he wanted to sound mad, not like he was serenading a lady.

"Wait. What?" I wasn't dreaming.

Denny backed away from the scene of the crime, past the bald patch bushes of heartbreak, and made his way down the front walk. I ran after him and caught him by the arm.

"Wait."

"It's been two weeks. No calls. Nothing."

"I'm sorry. I've been busy."

His words came out like an angry song. "You've never asked about my other friends. Not once. You never said, *Denny, why do you always invite Wayne on a plane to the mall? Where are your friends from your own school? Where are your friends from your synagogue?* You never asked me that!"

"Why would I?"

"Why didn't you?"

"Well, I don't know."

"I don't have other real friends, Wayne. I go to school just to get through it. News flash. I don't talk at school."

Man, the hurt in his eyes knocked me back. I wished he'd punched me. It would have hurt less.

"Because I don't have any. Not like you, Wayne. So now that you got your voice back, you ditch me? I mean, you were my friend. My *friend* friend. My parents were starting to think I was normal. Normal-ish."

I'd tried so hard to block out any thoughts that I'd even blocked out a good friend. Which, I realized, was a stupid move.

"Did you know that Wayne Kovok is an idiot?"

That made him smile. "So what's going on?"

"Sandy dumped me. My grandpa is sick—like, disease sick. And my mom's depressed."

"Is that all?"

"Try to contain your jealousy about my life."

"It'll be hard, but I'll try."

"Who made this pie?" I asked, detecting a strong banana-cream flavor.

"My mom."

"It tastes good. What I had of it, at least." I thought of her ambitious sandwiches and how now I might be able to eat one of them.

We stood there, not saying anything. No, there wasn't anything else to say. It would be all about action now. "Can you skateboard, Denny?"

"Like a boss!"

"Ask your mom if you can stay."

In two minutes, we were back on track, like nothing had gone wrong. The tightness in my chest eased a little.

I ran inside, raced into the garage, and grabbed my old, old skateboard.

I crashed into Grandpa as he was coming into the living room.

"Are you rabid, boy?" he said.

"Pie attack, sir." I turned to Denny, who was now standing right behind me, grinning. "Friendly fire."

"Pie, you say? Any left?"

"Negative."

"Okay then, carry on."

CHAPTER 29

Spring was coming fast and green and I was actually looking forward to spring break. It was the next week.

The Flee sent me a text: I'll try and get by to see you. We'll go to a concert or something.

I didn't bother replying.

I hadn't seen him since my awful birthday. And do you know what? I didn't care. I wasn't about to be a chump. Because do you know how many concerts I've *almost* attended? Too many to count. It's depressing.

Besides, Denny and I had plans to go to the movies and hang out all spring break. Lately, we'd go sit in the kiosk of Elegant Engravings after school and help Mrs. Rosenblatt with orders or play Minecraft. The mall wasn't a bad place to be, really. There were distractions every ten minutes.

Families shopping together. Couples holding hands. Miserable girls trailing behind their fathers into the shoe store. Even more miserable boys following their mothers into the candle store. I even spotted the trio of gymnasts from West Academy. They walked past me, each with her hair pulled up in a ponytail. Each with a different-colored ribbon. Red. White. And blue.

"Hey, Wayne," they said as they breezed past the kiosk.

"Hey," I replied.

And Denny sprang into action with song. "Wayne, are you going to introduce me?"

I punched him in the shoulder. "Those gymnasts are out of your league."

"Gymnasts?" He said that with a big smile on his face.

"Boys, why don't you walk around," Mrs. Rosenblatt suggested. "Go get a soda or something." She shoved some cash into Denny's palm and we left.

When we got back, we decided to play Minecraft again. Before I launched the game, I discovered a new alert in my e-mail: New Flight 56 debris found in East Texas.

"Denny, get over here."

It was a video news report. Liz Delaney standing by the side of some road. We watched the report seventeen times.

True story.

"This is Liz Delaney, reporting live for KTSB-Three News. We're here on Highway Forty-Three in Karnack, Texas, just on the outskirts of Caddo Lake State Park, and if I can just get our cameraman to pan upward into this thicket of cypress trees. There, do you see that flapping up there in the trees? You can really see how the color red stands out, and that's what got the attention of local residents. We weren't sure what this item was until late yesterday.

"Sources tell us this is a piece of debris from the crash of Flight Fifty-Six late last year. A family member called our station, alerting us to the fact that this quilt belonged to Nelda White, resident of Shreveport. Ms. White, who perished in the crash, was on her way to see relatives. Ms. White's relatives recognized this as a Christmas tree skirt she had made for her family.

"Local officials will later bring a fire truck and cherry picker to access and then return the item to Ms. White's relatives. A poetic reunion. Back to you, Jeb."

A tree skirt flapping from the top of a tree? Something caught in the tops of tree branches a few miles from the existing debris field. My theory was correct! The tree skirt. The flag. They both had kite-like qualities and had sailed closer to Caddo Lake State Park. I knew it. I *knew* it! It was still out there, waiting to be found and precisely folded and placed into the empty display case. Returned to my grandfather and mother from a grateful nation.

So I could shout now. I could talk. I could even make a phone call to Liz Delaney of KTSB-3 News with my new, older-sounding voice and let her know that more debris was ready to be found.

I looked at Denny, and it was as if he'd read my mind. "Call her!" he shouted.

I found her number and called.

Know what the recording said?

This voice-mail box is full. Please try again later.

True story.

I couldn't wait to get home and put a pin on my debris-collection map. Denny and I watched the video again. We had to wait for Mrs. Rosenblatt to close up her shop.

"Come home and have dinner with us, Wayne," she said.

It was tough to pass up a delicious meal from Mrs. Rosenblatt.

"I've got to get home," I told her.

And when I did get home and go into my room to check my data, I found Grandpa standing there in front of my closet door, rubbing his chin, about to pronounce me a darn Kovok.

CHAPTER 30

He stared at my closet door of research.

All the little bullet points of facts and data. Missing things and found things and miracles and randomness.

My maps of East Texas.

The dots I'd placed at the NTSB search areas. The debris fields. The definitions of wind speed. Pictures of American burial flags and photos of our downed plane. My dry-erase board with my still-unsolved science project hypothesis. All my notes in a neat pile on my desk. I tried to look at the door the way a stranger might look at it.

Viewed from that perspective, it only looked like a mess of papers and tape.

So any words to describe my project had to be carefully selected.

"Hi, Grandpa" was my carefully selected response. Not the best selection of words, mind you, but the only ones I could get out.

"Wayne."

A long, awkward silence. The kind I wanted to fill with a fact or even a statement about the weather.

"So, what are you doing in here?"

"Well, I found this on the computer printer and thought I'd bring it to you," Grandpa said.

He handed me a single sheet of paper. It was a list of medical miracles.

DATA

List of Medical Miracles

• *Two-year-old boy with cancerous tumor near spine. Day before his surgery, doctors find the tumor has vanished.*

• *Man injured in car accident wakes up from coma ten minutes before life support was to be turned off.*

One week later, says his first words to parents: "I love you."

• *An Irish woman with terminal cancer in her kidneys baffles doctors after her scans and X-rays show the tumors have disappeared, possibly attributed to her own immune system and fervent prayers.*

My throat cracked.

"Tell me what we're looking at here," he said, gesturing to the closet door.

I took a deep breath. "These are maps of East Texas. The red dots show where the NTSB has searched, and the yellow pins show where someone found a piece of the wreckage."

"And the area circled in pencil?"

"Caddo Lake State Park. The area no one has searched because it's too far east and out of the estimated debris field. But look at this."

I showed him the video about Nelda White's found tree skirt.

"Heavier objects were thrown from the plane, and the pull of gravity allowed them to land at a distance of about 17 miles from the crash site. My theory is that, with winds reported at fifty-plus miles per hour on the crash date, a four-pound, five-by-nine-and-a-half-feet cotton US burial flag might have taken on kite-like qualities and gone aloft farther east. Nelda White, the woman in 14A who sat next to us? The tree skirt and the flag went out of the plane simultaneously. They must have landed near each other."

"Quite a theory."

"Yes, sir."

"Let's just stand here and have a good, long look."

I didn't so much study the data as wait him out. He might compliment me or he might make fun of me. It could go either way.

"The weather forecast for this week is clear. Good driving weather, in fact. Good week for a road trip."

Grandpa's voice was as clear and confident as ever. His *don't argue with me* voice. His healthy, precancer voice. Still, I didn't know if he was serious. One thing I learned from having lost my voice was this: I'd made my voice say and do things that didn't match my mind. A lot. Lots of times when I'd uttered facts, my voice sounded more confident. Like the voice of another person.

"Your face is a question mark, son," Grandpa said.

"But...the liver?"

"Remember how I told you about Henry Dalton, who fought in the Revolutionary War? He died on the steps of his home. Got all the way home on foot after a long fight on the battlefield."

Mom walked in. "What's going on?"

"Planning a road trip," Grandpa said.

"What? A road trip?" she said.

Okay, I admit I was giddy. Happy. I'd been hoping for a chance to go east and explore areas even the NTSB and Liz Delaney hadn't considered.

So I said to her, "Mom! We're going to go and get Uncle Reed's flag! Even though, you know, it's sort of impossible."

True story.

"Isn't that like looking for a needle in a haystack?" Mom asked.

"Denny says it's the ultimate needle-in-a-haystack search."

"Well, my grandson has a theory," Grandpa said. "And so we're going to search or die trying."

"Dad!" Mom had her hands on her hips now.

"What? Oh, well…"

"Don't say stuff like that." Her voice sounded hurt.

"The person in the room with cancer can say whatever the Sam Hill he likes. It's a law!" His voice had laughter in it. In fact, he slapped his knee and laughed out loud. And it made me laugh. A little.

"It's not funny," Mom said, but she laughed a little, too. Then she got teary-eyed. "You can't. You can't go."

"Jennifer, we're going," Grandpa said. "Three days maximum, and then you can worry over me as much as you wish. Give me your silver bell and wait on me hand and foot. How about that?"

"I just don't know," Mom said. "Wayne?"

She said my name like a question. I looked at her straight on.

"Mom, do you trust me?"

"Wayne, honey, I trust you like I trust the sun will rise tomorrow."

"I'll take care of him. I will. Let me do this for you, okay?"

Then Grandpa took Mom by the shoulders and he hugged her tight. Sergeant Grandpa, the hugger.

"Hey, you raised him," he said. "He didn't get that stubborn streak from me."

Yes.

Mom swallowed hard. Her fear was trying to stomp out our plan. Her mind was racing, I could tell.

What if he gets sick?

What if they need a doctor?

What if? What if? What if?

Do you know what? *What if* is also a plaguing question.

DATA

Caddo Lake borders Texas and Louisiana.

It is the largest natural lake in the South.

Home to the world's largest cypress forest

Total of 26,810 acres of swamp

Items found from Flight 56 in the park = zero

Conclusion: Odds of finding the lost item are likely to match odds of being in a plane crash = 1 in 1.2 million.

CHAPTER 31

The next morning, Grandpa drank hot tea and seemed to come alive with the force of a confident drill sergeant.

Or, just like Grandpa.

I walked into the kitchen and caught him dancing with energy.

"Hurry up, Wayne."

I filled a bottle with water and packed a bunch of snacks in my backpack.

Mom came in, holding the phone in her hand. "Wayne, our neighbors are calling around to see if anyone knows about the decorative snowman on their porch. Know anything about that?"

I looked away from her and scanned the kitchen. My eyes landed on her blue glass birds.

"Did you know that the color blue is thought to help a person solve creative problems and that people are more productive in blue rooms?"

"Mmhmm. Just as I thought," Mom said.

Within minutes, we had Grandpa's old truck packed. We were soldiers on a mission. Like we were just going to walk into the woods and point to it. *There it is! Can't you see it?*

"You'll call as soon as you get there?" she asked.

"Of course," Grandpa said, swinging his duffel bag up over his arm. It seemed like his sickness had vanished. He wasn't complaining or sleeping or wearing a worried look on his face.

"Soldier, you ready to head out?"

"Yes, sir."

"Flashlight? Pocket knife? Compass?"

"Check."

"Clean white shirt? Success loves preparation. You never know when a clean shirt will be needed."

I went to my room for a clean white shirt.

And we were off. Driving east in the pale morning light. Plane lights blinking above and car headlights twinkling in the distance. We covered miles and miles of road without stopping or saying anything. Even our posture in the cab of his truck was tilted forward, as if the lean of our bodies would help us get there faster. About an hour in, I could see Grandpa twisting around in his seat, trying to get comfortable.

"I need to stop. Restroom break."

"Gee, Wayne, you've got the bladder of a little girl."

He exited the highway.

"That looks good." It was an old, beat-up-looking café. Harry's Café. We went inside and sat at the counter.

I went to the restroom, and when I returned, there were two mugs on the counter.

"That's yours," he said, pointing to a steaming cup of coffee. "If I can't enjoy it, you can. Ha!" He patted me on the back, and I sat down in front of the cup. Some guy walked over with a plastic bear full of honey and handed it to Grandpa. His name tag read HARRY, and his appearance matched his name.

"Anything else?" Harry asked as he looked at me. "Hope that coffee doesn't stunt your growth."

I took a couple of bitter sips. It tasted like brown salt.

"It'll put some vim and vigor in your bones, Wayne."

"I can't believe you love this stuff."

"Less of a love. More of a habit. Remember to separate the two in your mind if you can. Many an unwise person has fallen in love with his habits."

"I know what you're doing."

"What am I doing?"

"Trying to pelt me with all your knowledge."

"Says the boy with a university of facts in his head." He tousled my hair. An actual hair tousle. Who was this guy?

Back on the road, Grandpa turned up the truck's radio.

By lunchtime, we turned off the highway and headed north toward Karnack, right on the border of Caddo Lake State Park. Where the tree skirt of Nelda White in 14A had been recovered. Cruising down the two-lane stretch of highway, surrounded on both sides by tall, dark green pine trees so thick that daylight couldn't shine through, I revisited the logic of our mission.

It was void of logic.

Epically so.

Looking out on that forest, you realized how anything could get lost in those trees. A herd of yellow elephants could be hidden in there and you wouldn't know it.

Even though I wanted everything to make sense, I tried to shake off the notion that there was nothing scientific about this whole trip. The steps to our process consisted of (1) drive east, (2) get out of car, and (3) look around.

New topic.

"Did you know that a California couple struck gold while out walking their dogs?"

"Is that so?" Grandpa asked.

"They found two old buckets full of gold coins. Just on a walk, they became rich."

We turned off the main road and drove up a path near a cabin Grandpa had rented, just a half mile from where Nelda White's tree skirt had caught in the trees.

"Never guess the name of this town, Wayne."

"What?"

"Uncertain. We have arrived in Uncertain, Texas. How d'you like them apples?"

Weeks ago, when Uncertain, Texas, was a tiny red pin dot on my map, I'd looked up the origins of the name. The town of Uncertain is right on the Caddo Lake shoreline. The town got its name years ago when surveyors tried to determine the true border between Texas and Louisiana. They were uncertain about which side of the state line they were on. The word stuck.

I could see the happy thoughts form behind Grandpa's eyes. I didn't want to ruin his moment by blurting out those facts. But if you want to know, I was blazing with hope, too. The town's name made me more *certain* that Reed's flag was hiding here. Wasn't it the kind of detail Uncle Reed loved to include in his great true stories? It was almost like he was winking at us, daring us to go into the giant cypress forest with nothing and emerge with found treasure.

CHAPTER 32

Grandpa burst into my cabin room before dawn. I'm not kidding when I say *burst*, because the force of his entrance made the door hit the wall and left a dent.

"What? What time is it?"

"Get dressed. We're burning daylight."

"But there's no daylight yet!"

Outside the cabin, it smelled green. The sky was edged with light. Grandpa checked his compass.

"Good day! I can feel it," he said. "I've packed our provisions and water. Grab that orange backpack and binoculars." His voice was powerful. I wondered if this was the voice his soldiers got to hear all those years ago.

Our cabin was situated in the midst of other cabins, each maybe two hundred feet from the other. We headed away from the cabins and down a path marked with stumps and etched numbers. Mile 1.5. The ground was thick with leaves and rocks. Grandpa found a sturdy branch and used it as a walking stick.

"Always protect your feet. If your feet are fine, you are fine."

The first knowledge pelt of the day.

I found a branch of my own. It was handy to have a stick to feel out the path ahead. And we continued, walking through twisted and craggy cypress trees and brush. A sweet smell hung in the air, and morning light awakened everything. Birds sang. Leaves rustled. We marched. I got lost in the unfamiliar, beautiful woods and the steady *step-crunch-step-crunch* of my feet. But no signs of red or blue in the trees. Just thick drapes of olive-green Spanish moss.

"See anything?" Grandpa asked.

"Nope."

"Did you know that in 1861, during the Civil War, Captain William Driver sewed his twenty-four-star Union flag into his bedcovers so that Confederate forces descending upon Nashville couldn't take it from him? Flags can be hidden in unusual places, Wayne."

Knowledge pelt number two.

I gazed up at the trees just as a plane emerged from

the branches. My hand automatically went up into the air and carried it, and I told the passenger in seat 14A hello.

"Did you happen to see that guy who delivered and installed your mother's new dishwasher? His truck was spotless. Never do business with a man who has a dirty truck. The way a man keeps his ride tells you a lot about how he keeps his books."

Pelt.

"Grandpa?"

"Yeah?"

"I wish things were different."

And that made the air around us awkward.

And silent.

"Think we'll find the flag?" I asked finally.

"Maybe. Maybe not."

Just then, a park ranger drove past. His truck was scuffed and muddy and blended into the woods.

"I also wanted to tell you that there's a correct way to edge the grass. Straight, deep cuts an inch from the sidewalk."

"That's random."

"Isn't everything?" He was smiling when he said that.

"I guess."

"Your great-grandfather, RB Dalton, taught me all

these things, you know. A great student of history, that man. Always said a young boy needed to fill himself with knowledge and passion. Empty vessels get filled with the wrong things."

Pelt. Pelt. Pelt.

"What does *RB* stand for?" I asked. "You never told me."

"His name was a problem. His mother named him RB from birth, God knows why. But the United States Army requires a full name, no abbreviations. So he had to fill out all his forms *R-only B-only*. He went through the service called Ronly Bonly Dalton." Grandpa laughed. "When he got out of the service, he was so sick of it that he decided to call himself Howard."

"Howard?"

"That's where you get your middle name."

I'd never been a fan of my name. And now to know I was partially named after Ronly Bonly Dalton? Well, let's just say I would've changed my name, too.

"Glad I'm not totally named after him."

We stood at the edge of the water. A little sunlight shone on its surface. It was so quiet and beautiful. We walked out onto a dock and scanned the trees for uncommon colors. Once again, they gave back greens and grays. Nothing red, white, or blue.

I lost track of time. I just followed him. By the time

we made it back to the cabin, we were tired and silent and flagless.

The next morning, we headed out in the opposite direction from the previous day, winding through the tall cypress and pine trees.

"Tired?" I asked Grandpa.

"Not too much."

But he was.

"Just wishing Reed was with us. That boy could find a whisper in a whirlwind."

We walked alongside the banks of the lake. The water was a pea-green color and dotted with lily pads and dead cypress stumps. I turned my focus upward, adjusted the binoculars, and searched the treetops again.

I guess we'd walked for a while, looking skyward. I pressed my walking stick into the ground and kept moving. At one point, I almost lost sight of Grandpa. I turned around to find him about fifty yards behind me, perched on a rock. His whole body appeared heavy. It might have been time to quit the search for the day, if not forever.

I scanned the lake as if it might give up an answer. *Where should we go?*

The waters glimmered and sounded cool and reassuring, as if to say, *Come on in!*

"You gents need a ride?" A man not far from us was working on his boat next to a wooden dock. Along the dock, there was a sign: JOHNBOAT RENTALS. "Going fishing?" he asked.

"Yeah, but not for fish," I told him. "Can you give us a tour up Big Cypress Bayou and back? We're scanning the banks and trees."

"For what?"

For everything.

For all the missing treasures in the world.

For a needle in a haystack, otherwise known as an impossible adventure.

"Be right back," I said.

Soon enough, we were on the water, guided by the man who called himself Cap.

There were three bench seats inside the johnboat, and we sat behind Cap as he took off down Caddo Lake. In the center of the water, I scanned from the left and Grandpa searched to the right. The flag might have been deep in the woods, near the banks waiting for us, or nowhere.

There was only so much green I could look at. I wondered if anything could be found in this much thick spring green. Maybe if we'd come in another season when the trees were bare. That thought had tugged at me all morning. The only thing that gave me hope was that 14A's tree skirt had been found in this same season. I clung to that piece of data.

And the steady hum of the boat and the cool breeze off the river made us press on. It gave Grandpa a chance to rest. I worried that all his energy was used up. The liver causing its trouble again.

After a half hour of Cap telling us about alligators and waterfowl and a little history of the lake, he turned the johnboat backward and headed around a bend.

"Wait! There!" I said, pointing to a dock up ahead. All I could see was a patch of red. It stood out from the ten shades of green all around. And it sent a quickening through me. A flash of hope.

"Head over there, Cap," Grandpa said.

It was a perfect dock hanging over the murky water. Spanish moss draped from one side. There were two sets of steps descending into the bayou. A tin-roofed, fresh-painted double-wide a hundred yards beyond the water's edge. And smack-dab in the center of the dock was a pole flying Old Glory. An American flag. A flag picking up a little of the breeze.

Cap slowed the johnboat and then idled in front of the dock. "You spot a gator?"

"No," I said.

The flag was the standard-issue, gray-poled, eagle-topped kind you could find anyplace. Anywhere. Common. But seeing the red, white, and blue colors against the relentless green landscape refreshed my eyes the same way a cold glass of water refreshes the body.

"You gents all right? You look downright transfixed!" Cap said.

"We're fine," I said.

"It's just a flag. Retired army man named Broman lives up in that place. Meaner than a gator, that one. Got a pristine old car up in his shed he won't let you even whistle at to save your life."

Grandpa and I shared a look. "I knew a Broman in the army. Wouldn't be Eldon Broman?"

"Well, yes," Cap answered.

Before you could wink, Grandpa, Cap, and I were climbing onto the dock. Knocking on Eldon Broman's door and shaking hands.

"Sergeant Truman Dalton, the man who trained me," Broman said. "Do you know how brilliant this man is? Man, they are *still* talking about you! What brings you to Caddo Lake?" Broman was a younger version of Grandpa. He didn't seem meaner than a gator to me.

True story.

Grandpa rattled off the short but sad history of Uncle Reed's flag, including his "grandson's wild but intelligent theory" that the flag might be hiding among the cypress trees.

"Yeah, I heard about that crash," Broman said. "Really incredible."

"Well, we thought we'd come and have a look," Grandpa said.

"Seen anything?"

"Nope," I said.

"Well, I bet anything could hide in these woods in the spring," Broman offered. "Maybe in the fall, the flag would reveal itself. You could come back then. I'll help."

"Yes, maybe the fall would be a good season," Grandpa said. "We'd sure appreciate it if you could keep a lookout for it in the meantime."

"Sounds like my kind of mission," Broman said. "Hey, before you leave, come have a look at this."

Broman took us to his garage, lifted the gate, and unveiled—what else—a perfect car. It could have been a cousin of the Car. A shiny blue Dodge Charger.

Grandpa's eyes sparkled. "Would you look at that? It's the most beautiful Charger I've ever seen."

"What's the big deal about these old cars, anyway?" I asked.

Grandpa and Broman simultaneously shot me daggered looks. "Son, these are the cars we dreamed of in our youth. So when we got the chance to finally get them, we did," Broman explained.

"Speak for yourself, Broman. I got mine to impress a girl," Grandpa said, winking at me.

We said good-bye to Broman, and Cap took us back to his dock.

More than anything, I wanted to see Mom's face when I put the flag in her hands. More than anything. I hated that I didn't have it. That I didn't get it.

"I wanted to see your mom's face with that flag," Grandpa said. I don't know how he kept doing that. "Know what I think?"

"What?"

"I think it will be found in another season. Just like Broman said."

I swallowed hard. In another season, things might be different.

"And if it isn't found, well—" Grandpa broke off and stared up at the trees.

We walked silently back to the cabin, showered,

and decided to drive into town for something to eat. And nobody said it out loud, but we were going to see the crash site, too.

"Are you up for doing all this in one day?" I asked him.

"I'm hot, is all. Hot as a stolen tamale."

So we got back to the truck, cranked up the air-conditioning, and drove out to Route 69 and all the way to the crash site. To see it was like seeing some famous place. The field was charred and black. The tops of the pine trees were sheared off at different, exact points. It was like a perfect tree graph against the sky. And there wasn't a single house or barn for a mile in all directions. I wondered if the pilot had steered the plane to clear land to avoid crashing into anything but ground and trees. Or if by some unexplainable luck, the plane went down in an uninhabited place. It was a mystery for sure.

How Mom and I survived in the rush of the crash was a mystery, too. Standing there on the field, I just remember being stuck in the mud and seeing red emergency lights through the smoke.

The thought of all of it made me feel sad and lucky.

"You'll see things like this when you go into the army, Wayne," Grandpa said. "Things you can't explain."

"When I go into the army?"

302

"Yes."

"I wish people would stop saying that." I said it louder, angrier than I meant to. But I was annoyed. If you've ever gotten a bruise on your arm one day and then someone hits you on the exact same spot the next day, you will have an idea of what I felt like.

"Calm down."

I got out of the truck and leaned against the door. Grandpa got out, too, and came around the side of the truck. The sun was starting to go down.

Going into the army? Did you know that, to me, the idea of enlisting always felt like someone telling me to go hike a rocky mountain without any shoes on my feet? The idea seemed impossible. It looked painful. Failure likely. I wanted to scream, *Don't you see? I'm not prepared. I have no shoes.*

"Do you want to talk about it?" Grandpa asked.

"Not really."

"I think we should talk about it."

I waited. I wanted to talk. And I didn't want to talk.

"It's like everyone I know has this expectation of me. *Wayne, you should be a runner. Be a swimmer. Be a soldier!* When do I get a vote? What about letting me decide? What if I want to be a rock star?"

"You can sing?" he asked.

"That's not the point!"

"Okay, what's the point?"

"The point is I should get a vote. I mean, the Flee tells me I'm dumb if I'm not in a sport. That I need to be in track. And you and Mom. You assume I'll go join the army. What if I'm not cut out for it? What if it's just not me, you know? What if I want to decide myself?"

Grandpa squared his shoulders, fixed me with a look, and smiled.

"What? You think I'm funny?"

"No."

"Yes, you do. You're always laughing at me."

"I don't *always* laugh about anything."

"Never mind."

"But I am happy. Happy you found your voice. You're finding out how to take a stand for yourself. And I'm smiling because I'm glad I was here to see it."

"Whatever."

"You're going to be all right, Kovok. You know, even if you do rat-trap birds in your backyard."

It was the way he looked at me. With a genuine smile on his face.

"It was an accident," I said, trying to swallow a laugh. But it was no use. We were both about to crack up.

"Bird killer," he said.

"Old fart."

I took a deep breath.

I couldn't help but hug him. I couldn't help it.

"I wish things were different." My voice cracked.

"So do I." His voice cracked, too. He hugged me back.

Then we leaned against the truck and stared at the field where the plane had crashed. When the sun set, it looked peaceful.

"Know what I want?" Grandpa asked.

"A cheeseburger, sir." I might have wiped a tear from my face.

"Affirmative, Kovok."

"But you can't have a cheeseburger."

"I can watch someone enjoy a cheeseburger. Next best thing to eating one. My research tells me there is a restaurant in town called the Hamburger Store."

Grandpa ordered for me. He told me that ordering the burger and the anticipation of the burger was the next-best thing. Because I'd been forbidden to eat delicious food for a few months, I had to disagree with him. But what could I say?

He punched my arm and told me to describe the cheeseburger. Leave no detail unreported. I described the toasted, buttered bun in a way that would earn applause. I described the crunch of cold pickles and noted their contrast with the salty, juicy meat. I began a short poem on my love of the tomato but was interrupted by a scream.

More of a shout. A female shout.

"Oh. My. Gosh!"

Liz Delaney of KTSB-3 News was loud and bouncy and bright-lipsticked, even in person.

"You! I know you. Who are you?"

Liz Delaney? Asking me a question? I couldn't believe my ears.

"I'm the person who sent you more than ten e-mails. Wayne Kovok."

"What?"

"I sent you e-mails about plane debris from Flight Fifty-Six. You never responded."

"Did you spell my name with two *z*'s? If not, I bet your e-mail bounced. Happens to a lot of people who don't spell my name correctly."

I checked my e-mail from my phone, scanning my spam folder, and sure enough, it was clogged with bounced e-mails.

"But Liz with two *z*'s?"

"I know, right," she said. "Ask my mother. You have a

lot of choices in life, but you can't choose the name you're born with."

"I guess you could have changed it by now," I said.

"Yeah, but now I'm original and I like it."

Lizz Delaney dragged a chair from another table and plopped herself down with us. "And who is this hand-some guy?"

"Sergeant Truman Dalton, US Army, retired," Grandpa said.

"Lizz Delaney, sir." She pulled out her phone and began scrolling. "Okay, I know I've got it somewhere."

She put her phone in front of my face and shouted, "That's you, right? It's you! I've been looking for you."

I studied the picture.

It was the field on the day of the crash.

A downed plane. Everything wet. A fireball and smoke in the upper left corner. The hazy outline of people. Emergency workers.

And me.

Wayne Howard Kovok, running away from a giant airplane fireball, Mom in my arms.

Grandpa took the phone and studied it.

"I'll be darned, son," Grandpa said. "You must have run faster than double-struck lightning. You remember any of that?"

I wished I had a clear memory, but I could only remember being scared and stuck and unable to speak and Mom needing help.

"No, sir. Not really."

"We'll be needing a copy of that photo, Ms. Delaney," Grandpa said. "Say, let's shoot out the lights and get you a cheeseburger!"

"Excuse me?" she said.

"My grandfather is asking if you'd like to celebrate," I offered. "He has a way with words."

"Of course, then! Now, Wayne, please, please let me interview you. Can you come back next week?"

I looked at Grandpa. "I have to get back to school."

"Okay then, wait a few minutes." She dashed away.

Before you knew it, there were bright, hot lights set up outside the Hamburger Store and Lizz Delaney was holding a microphone, making a short speech about the facts of the crash, summing it all up in about two minutes before turning to me and asking questions.

"You said you didn't remember getting to safety?"

"That's right. It was all so fast."

"And now we know you carried your mother to safety. That's pretty brave."

"I don't know. I reacted. I ran away from danger. Isn't that what anyone would do?"

I was getting nervous with her questions and wanted it to be over. The fact-spitting part of me was pushing its way up.

Don't say Frankenbuckettia! Don't say Frankenbuckettia!

"It's been months since the accident. How are you doing now? Are you okay, Wayne?"

I would like to tell you that I was the best interviewee that ever existed. That my first and only TV interview somehow rose to the top of the YouTube charts and made me famous and renowned.

I would like to tell you that I didn't freeze when Lizz Delaney asked that question. Her eyes and the bright camera lights, asking me to tell them everything was okay.

That question that I didn't know how to answer.

I guess I wanted to say that okay had nothing to do with it. I was different. Was different the same as okay?

"Yeah, I'm okay," I said finally.

"We're so happy to hear that, Wayne, and we wish you and your family all the best."

"Oh, one more thing," I said.

"Of course," Lizz Delaney replied.

I waved into the camera. "Hi, Denny!"

That last night in the cabin, we got to bed early. The trip hadn't been anything like what I'd imagined. It didn't matter that we didn't have the flag. No, that's a lie. It did matter. I wanted to be the one to find it. Part of me still wanted to walk every inch of East Texas until it was found. And maybe someday I'd do that. The mystery would always make me think about what it was like BEFORE and then AFTER.

CHAPTER 33

Six weeks later on Cedar Drive, two big guys delivered a special hospital bed on a Saturday and set it up in our living room. We moved the flowery couch into the garage to make space. A home health nurse pulled up behind the delivery truck and started up the walk.

"No waterworks," Grandpa said.

"Yes, sir."

"It's just a bed."

"Did you know the first mattresses were stuffed with pea pods as their filling?"

"Nope, can't say that I knew that." What Grandpa had said was that he'd had a good life and he wanted a good death. And that meant being around the people he cared about and not a bunch of nurses and strangers. That was what he said, so we all agreed.

I tried to look at the bed as just a bed. I tried to look at the home health nurse as just a friendly visitor.

But I couldn't.

I read somewhere that the heart and the brain are only eighteen inches apart inside the body. Well, it was hard for my head to send down the message to my racing heart that the arrival of a bed meant time was running out.

So I called Denny. Mrs. Rosenblatt pulled up to the curb an hour later with Denny and a giant soup pot.

Mrs. Rosenblatt shouted from her car, "For your family! Bubbie's recipe. Take it inside, Denny."

Denny shoved the giant soup pot into my hands.

"Bubbie's recipe? So it probably has a lot of fiber, right?"

"It'll drop on you like a stomach bomb," Denny sang.

"Great."

We got into Mrs. Rosenblatt's van and headed away from Cedar Drive, where no one had to see a big, comfy hospital bed in the middle of the living room. We were going to hang out at the mall.

Denny whispered to me, "Wayne, did you know that one of the world's largest matzo balls weighed four hundred and twenty-six pounds, was made with more than seventeen hundred eggs, and was created in 2010 for a Jewish food festival? Although, technically, it was not the world's largest ball, because it was not recorded by Guinness World Records. Guinness lists the largest matzo ball at only two hundred sixty-seven pounds and made with about a thousand eggs."

I glared at him.

"W-w-what? You like facts when you're nervous. So I gave you facts."

At the mall, we went to Denny's latest hangout. Lady Foot Locker.

"Does your mother know you're like this?"

"She thinks I'm an angel."

I punched him solid, but he just laughed.

We got back to Elegant Engravings, and Mrs. Rosenblatt asked us to "man the store" so that she could go grab a sandwich. I sat down on the floor of the kiosk and opened my laptop. Denny kicked me.

"What?"

And there she was. Monica. The pretty, dark-eyed girl from Denny's bar mitzvah. I could see her through the glass cases of the kiosk.

Denny looked at me, helpless.

"Hi, Denny," Monica said. "I really like that song you sang. Are you a Beatles fan?"

Denny looked down at me again. Quickly, I wrote a small note and held it up for him to read.

"Monica, did you know that the first lyrics to the Beatles' hit song 'Yesterday' were 'Scrambled eggs'?" he sang.

"Really? That's cool," Monica said. I gave Denny a thumbs-up.

Mrs. Rosenblatt came back, so we decided to walk around the mall because Denny was so pumped up about Monica.

"She's really pretty, isn't she?" Denny asked. "And she likes the Beatles. Perfect."

That was when I spotted another pretty girl.

Sandy Showalter, leaning against the giant panda in front of Panda Palace. Her long blond hair? Gone. All cut off in some short style. She was surrounded by ordinary girls with ordinary hair. But she was the most beautiful. Still.

"*Hola*, Señor Kovok." Sandy ran over.

"*Cómo estás?*"

"Call me, Wayne? We can hang out."

Did you know that when you lose your voice and can't talk, your hearing gets sharper and the way you pay attention to sounds is different? Some words sound harsh and mean. Some, worried and sad. And some just sound so beautiful.

Call me, Wayne? We can hang out.

Those were really beautiful words.

True story.

"Sure. I'll call you. We'll hang out."

Denny and I walked around for a while and ended up in Macy's, where he went through the cologne gauntlet. Again. But the cologne ladies with their white jackets reminded me of nurses. And nurses reminded me of hospital beds. So much for going to the mall and distracting myself.

I didn't know I'd gone outside the Macy's exit doors until the rain hit me in the face like a slap. The rain had come out of nowhere. It wasn't even in the day's weather forecast.

Sort of like the way I was feeling. It came out of nowhere, too.

"W-W-Wayne, w-wait up!"

"Did you know that seventy-five percent of your brain is water?" I asked.

"Inside, please," Denny said.

"Denny, did you know that a sneeze exceeds one hundred miles per hour? It does. A cough clocks in at about sixty miles per hour. How about your nose? Want to know something about your nose? It can remember fifty thousand scents, so you're filling it up with cologne. Feet? Feet have five hundred thousand sweat glands. Your facial hair grows faster than any other hair on the body, so you'd better invest in a good razor, Denny. Your fingernails? They grow four times faster than toenails. The fastest-growing nail is on the middle finger. And—"

"Wayne!" He had to scream.

"Yeah?"

And he returned to his whisper-voice that kept the stutters away. "What's wrong, Wayne on a plane?"

"Nothing."

"So, what? Sandy?"

"No, it's not Sandy."

"Then what?"

"I don't want to look at pretty girls in the mall anymore, okay?" My words came out quick and angry. It showed on Denny's face. "Look, I don't want to be mean, but I didn't like Sandy because she was nice to look at. I liked her because she was Sandy. I liked her because when we did the Alamo project together, she was smart and creative and remembered to put a few girl action figures next to the Alamo. And also, that story I told about the ketchup."

"Not every girl would rescue a ketchup-faced nerd. I'm a dope."

"You're not a dope."

316

"Agreed. Something else bothers Wayne on a plane, yes?"

"It's just…"

"You love him."

"Shut up."

I was glad I was out in the rain.

"You. *Love. Him!*"

"Shut *up!* Let's both shut up, all right?"

"Sometimes that's impossible. For you. The awkward silences are the blanks. Wayne Kovok fills in the blanks of life. Leave no fact unturned, Wayne on a plane!"

"When are you going to stop calling me that?"

"When I stop stuttering."

Denny Rosenblatt was right more than he was wrong. My discomfort with the blank spaces made me aware of how much I didn't know. How much I couldn't control or change. "Okay, the brain," I said.

"Yeah, the brain?"

"It consumes more oxygen than any other organ in the human body," I said to him. "Deep breaths keep your brain happy and alert."

"Keep going."

"Did you know that *Jeopardy!* first aired in 1964?

"Did you know that the author of *The Wizard of Oz* got the name of the magical land in his books by looking at the drawers of a filing cabinet? He scanned A–G, H–N, and then O–Z, and chose it."

I filled in the blanks until Mrs. Rosenblatt closed up the Elegant Engravings kiosk and splashed up to the curb at the mall and honked.

"Oh, honey, you look hungry to me," she said. "I will make you a sandwich."

I finally got to eat one of Mrs. Rosenblatt's ambitious sandwiches.

And I told her that it banished my craving for Beatty Middle School cafeteria pizza sticks forever. That was the biggest compliment a sandwich ever got.

CHAPTER 34

I still hadn't seen the Flee. In fact, I didn't think about him until he'd text me about coming over. I always said I was busy. Then I got the scowl from Mom.

"He's trying, honey," she'd say. "I sent him that Lizz Delaney story. He's proud of you."

Yeah, I'd like to *hear* that.

Well, I had school. Going to the mall after school with Denny. Watching TV with Grandpa at night. My schedule had no room for anything else. His doctor had told us that Grandpa would have good days and bad days. And then it would change to good hours and bad hours. I didn't want to miss anything.

I preferred sitting in front of the TV with Grandpa. Mr. Darcy, sitting on the floor underneath the giant bed.

We watched shows about D-Day. About Vietnam.

We watched cooking shows. We even watched a Jane Austen film with Mom.

Grandpa rearranged himself on the bed and ordered me to reheat his water bottle.

His back hurt. He lost weight. He drank hot water or this gross herbal tea Mom read about that was supposed to help.

Know what the tea looked like? Like the same going into the body as it did coming out.

Know what it smelled like? It's that same rotten smell that punches you in the face when you've left a salad in your fridge too long.

Still, he drank the putrid concoction. A lot of days, he ordered me to go jog around the block; no grandson of his was going to be soft. Then he would wink at me.

"Unless it's your decision to be soft," he said.

I wasn't going to be soft.

After dinner, I usually ran down Cedar Drive. Past the hulking water tower. Past the forest of trees and into the Estates.

When I got back home, I'd shower and then we'd watch a TV marathon, but I couldn't tell you what was on. We always talked over the sound.

That was how most days went as we headed toward summer.

On the first Tuesday of June, Mom made a cake.

Did you know that Mom hadn't made a cake in a year? When she made cake, it was a celebration.

"Are we celebrating?" Grandpa asked.

"The premiere of Tim's new commercial is going to air tonight," she said.

"Well, hot diggity," Grandpa said.

Tim LeMoot came over and we all ate spaghetti around Grandpa, which I thought was a little mean, but he said he didn't mind. Then the commercial came on and there was Tim LeMoot, on the screen, in the middle of a giant field.

You need an attorney who is outstanding in his field. Call me, TIM LEMOOT, THE TEXAS BOOT. I'M OUT STANDING IN MY FIELD!

It was hilarious. Everyone said so.

"Wasn't that hilarious?" Mom asked. Tim and Mom went to the kitchen and cleaned up.

That night, I would have sworn Grandpa looked a shade of yellow. Not one of the good days. He was in pain and he took his medications. I had a knowing feeling that night. Something pushed at me. Something told me we were down to the good hours.

Say it. Say it. Say it!

"I love you."

"Love you, too, son."

Silence. Not awkward, but the relieving kind. Like when you've been holding your breath and you let out a sigh.

"So, you gonna rat-trap some birds tomorrow?" His voice was low and ragged.

"You gonna eat my sandwich and then stink up the place?"

"Darn Kovok."

"Old fart."

He fell asleep. But I didn't move. I didn't want to move. What if it was the *last* good hour?

Before Grandpa drifted off to sleep, he whispered, "Hank Williams needs a girlfriend."

"How about Dolly Parton?"

"Son, I was thinking the exact same thing." He closed his eyes and fell asleep. The forever kind. I don't know how I knew it, but I did. For so long, things had been awkward and annoying between us. But do you know what? Right before he died, I was the happiest I'd ever been in my life. I was grateful I'd been in a plane crash. I got to see my grandfather every single day for months. If that plane hadn't plummeted, we would have stalled at spaghetti Tuesdays.

And that's the truth.

Later the next morning, people from the funeral home came into our house and rolled out a stretcher holding the best man I ever knew.

The house felt huge and empty without him. He'd filled it.

I went to my room and played video games so that I wouldn't have to think about anything.

Later, Mom and I watched a movie and Tim LeMoot came over with pizza and flowers, and Mrs. Rosenblatt and Denny came over with brisket and bread, and Mom cried more.

And I cried more, too. I admit it.

And when I went into the kitchen and saw Mom's blue glass birds on the counter, I almost lost it. I lined them up like soldiers. I looked out the kitchen window to fill up my eyes with blue sky so that they wouldn't fill up with anything else.

And I didn't ask God why I was in the random plane crash that caused Grandpa to come and live with us.

I just bit my lip and said, *Thank you*.

True story.

CHAPTER 35

I couldn't be in our living room. It was still too full of an empty bed. People were eating casseroles or brisket sandwiches made by Mrs. Rosenblatt.

So I sat on our couch in the garage staring at a pristine 1967 Mustang in case the tears came. Because they were trying hard to make an appearance.

We'd buried Grandpa hours earlier.

He'd wanted a standard military graveside service.

Right next to the love of his life, a girl he'd met at the hardware store.

A soldier played taps. Grandpa's coffin was draped in a five-by-nine-and-a-half-feet, four-pound cotton American flag, precisely refolded by soldiers wearing white gloves.

They presented it to my mother. And me.

She wept.

Tim LeMoot, the Texas Boot, held her up.

And Denny sang, but not because I asked him to. Because he remembered Grandpa telling him he could sing at the funeral if he sang a song Grandpa liked called "Tell My Father," which I thought had been a joke, but which Denny took as an order. He sang it so well that I had to bite the inside of my cheek to keep from crying. I swear to you that the planes stopped flying overhead and the world paused and saluted a great patriot.

It was beautiful and incredible. Like chill-bumps-on-a-hot-day incredible.

Man, Denny Rosenblatt was born to sing. Grandpa would have liked it.

I don't know when the service was officially over. I'd trained my eyes to stay focused on the fake green carpet they put on the ground near Grandpa's burial site. I had to let my eyes fill up with green.

Green. Green. Green.

I guess I stared at the ground for a long time.

Denny had to nudge me out of my fog.

Denny whispered, "Out with it."

"What?" I asked.

"I know you. You have that classic Wayne-needs-to-unload-a-fact look."

"I have a look?"

"More of an odor, really. Like I can smell it coming."

"It's nothing."

"Come on," Denny whispered. "You'll be factually constipated if you don't get it out!"

It wasn't a fact that weighed on my mind. Nothing like that.

I said to Denny, "I was just thinking I'm glad you didn't wear too much cologne today."

Denny and I walked to the car and rode back to Cedar Drive.

And I lined up the series of events in my life that had led me here.

Maybe if Reed hadn't been raised to be a soldier, he wouldn't have joined the army.

And he wouldn't have protected his unit in battle and died for them.

We wouldn't have gone to his funeral.

And returned on a plane that crashed.

And lost my voice and a flag.

And found a friend with a unique voice.

And been taken care of by a patriot.

Who was getting sick.

And needed his daughter and grandson.

And one last mission and a good death.

I got Denny. A chance to really know Grandpa. Even photographic evidence of Wayne Kovok running on auto-pilot, being fearless and brave.

Mom hung my photo on the wall across from the Wall of Honor.

"I'm starting a new wall!" she said.

"What are you going to call it?"

"The Wall of Honor, Part Two. How's that?"

Now Grandpa's picture would stare at me forever. His picture on the Wall of Honor was next to Uncle Reed's. But Mom? She was crazy happy about a wall. Again. I liked her crazy happy.

"It's perfect, Mom," I told her.

So after the funeral, I hid out in the garage and let my eyes fill up with the Car.

The perfect car.

I stared and stared until the red gleam was impossibly shiny. Until I saw a letter on the dashboard. A letter addressed to me.

Dear Wayne,

We said most things in life. There's not much left to say, but I want you to have it in pen and ink that I think you are a straight arrow. Did you know I'm proud of you, Wayne?

So proud. Proud of the way you respond to the world when she hits you upside the head. She's going to do that to you, you know. There's no getting around it. But as I've told you in different ways, it's the way a man responds that is the true measure of his worth. You tell your own sons and daughters that, Wayne. Names don't mean anything. You taught me that. So you tell them my stories and the stories of our family. We need more Wayne Kovoks in the world. You look after your mother. Take care of Hank Williams, too. Remember me when you eat a cheeseburger. Especially one with heavy pickle.

The Car is yours.

At ease, son,
Grandpa

There may have been waterworks.

There may have been a waterfall of waterworks.

Okay, there was an unstoppable force of tears.

They leaked even though I was smiling at the same time.

How did he make me do that? Smile and cry.

"Hey, are you okay?" It was Mom.

I stood up straight and rubbed the side of the Car with the hem of my shirt. "Yeah. Yeah."

"Nice car you got there, huh?" she said.

"You knew?"

"I knew."

"Hey, did you know that the thing you have to remember with old cars is that they don't just start up cold as soon as you turn the key? You have to pump the gas twice and then hold down the pedal."

CHAPTER 36

Now it was July and school was out. Denny hung out with me on Cedar Drive. Sandy and I texted *en español*. And I sat in the Car a lot. Sometimes I'd sit there reading and when I'd find an interesting fact, I'd read it aloud. Or sometimes I'd text a fact to Sandy, Mysti, and Rama. I couldn't help it. I have the blood of nerds *and* Revolutionary War heroes running through my veins. I figure I'm a Revolutionary Nerd.

And I was fine with that. But something was still missing, and it had nothing to do with the flag. I had traveled so far. Gone to another country. Finally earned my citizenship. I guess I wanted to keep moving forward. Keep using my new voice.

So on the first Saturday of July, I called the Flee.

Mom and Tim LeMoot were in the kitchen getting ready to grill cheeseburgers for lunch, and I started to feel feelings.

About a cheeseburger.

New topic.

Did you know Debra LeMoot, daughter of the Texas Boot, was in my kitchen, too?

"Debra, this is Wayne," Tim LeMoot said. "Wayne's hobbies include fact-finding, skateboarding, and redesigning inflatable snowmen."

Tim LeMoot smiled at me and winked.

Debra LeMoot had hair the color of a shiny penny and wanted to work at her dad's law practice.

She did not recoil when she met seventh graders with scarred faces.

She was also a nice distraction from the sadness of cheeseburgers.

I was supposed to help her with the salad, but then I remembered I needed to feed Hank Williams. That was when I saw the Flee get out of his car.

He was about two hours earlier than I'd told him to arrive, which was strange for the Flee. I'm sure he thought it was about the money. I don't know how the Flee thought he was entitled to any portion of the airline settlement all that time. His brain just worked that way. I knew his brain also worked in other odd ways. Maybe he had the kind of brain that liked messing with people he thought were weak and scared and wimpy.

So I finished feeding Hank Williams and then I fed Dolly Parton.

And then, because I'm an action-oriented person like my grandfather, I got ready for a mission. I just had to get past Mom and the Texas Boot. They were deep into a conversation about movies.

As it turned out, Tim LeMoot was also a Jane Austen fan and has watched many movies with Mom. (How do you say *ugh* with a British accent?)

Or maybe he just knew how to be a good boyfriend and be interested in what his girlfriend liked. Anyway, he made Mom happy and he showed up when he said he was going to show up.

Those were two things I liked in a person.

Do you know when it's fun to watch TV with Mom and Tim LeMoot? It's when the Tim LeMoot commercial appears. I challenged him to a dare the other night.

I dare you to mute the TV and perform the commercial with a British accent, I said.

And he did. Tim LeMoot stood up and said, *I would*

very much like to kick the money into your pocket, if you please, and I'm terribly, terribly sorry that you've been in a serious auto accident.

It was the funniest thing I'd seen in weeks. That was, until I saw the Flee coming up the walk wearing a T-shirt that said WINNER in bright, bold blue letters. As far as I knew, he hadn't won anything for years.

True story.

The doorbell rang before I could reach the door.

"Doug, I already told you to please call *before* you come by," Mom said.

"For your information, Wayne called me. Told me to bring my running shoes so we could jog or something."

"Is that a fact?" Mom asked.

"That's a fact," I said, pushing through Mom and Tim LeMoot.

"Wayne, what's going on?" Mom asked.

"Mom, did you know that before you take the bull by the horns, you should make sure it's your bull?"

I made her smile. A good fact will do that to a person. And my mom had a great smile.

"Yes, I think someone once told me that, Wayne."

"This is my bull now." I kissed her head and opened the door. My bull was in the front yard doing stretches that could've frightened squirrels and small children.

"So, you wanted to talk to me? Run or something?"

I nodded.

"Wayne, don't waste my stupid—"

"I have something to say to you!" I interrupted.

"Well, say it."

We were the exact same height now. Exactly the same. Our eyes were level. Straight on. My stomach quaked a little, I admit. But I'd practiced my words. I wasn't going to let another summer go by without speaking my mind.

"When I see your face sometimes, I see the red taillights of your car. I see myself scared. Terrified. Alone. You laughing and leaving me behind. I don't like what I see. I don't want to see that anymore. What you did was full-out wrong."

"What?"

"You heard me."

He broke eye contact with me then, but I held firm, looking straight at the top of his head.

"I didn't realize that."

"Well, now you do."

"So, what is this?"

"I guess I'd just like an apology, Dad."

He shuffled his feet and looked at the ground.

His voice turned low. "I didn't realize all that, Wayne. I'm sorry. I'm no parenting expert."

True story.

"Don't do that to Carrot, either. When I come over, he'd better be a happy kid. And I'm thinking of going out for track and field next year, but I'll let you know what I decide."

The Flee smiled a little. "We'd like it if you came over."

I put my hand out for him to shake. "I'm going to come over."

"I'm sorry, Wayne. Real sorry." My dad shook my hand.

"And I would like you to stop saying you're just messing with me. For the record, I do *not* like to be messed with."

"Well, any more requests, then?"

"You brought your running shoes, didn't you?"

"Have you been practicing? Are you going to outrun me?"

"Maybe."

Definitely.

"What's gotten into you? You've changed!"

Truer story.

"Well, I'm proud of you, you know. Proud of the young man you're becoming."

I was about to spit out a fact about rubber-soled shoes. I was about to. I'm glad I didn't.

"Okay, let's go," I said, and I took off down Cedar Drive.

The sky was clear blue, and the July sun wasn't too hot. I fell into a solid pace, my feet beating out a heartbeat against the cracks along the sidewalk. Our pace was matched as we turned up onto the smooth streets of the Estates, running side by side in unison. I stepped up my pace as the street rose and fell. The tall cottonwood trees of the park swayed in the distance over the rocket ship. After another half mile, I tuned out his complaining. All I heard was the wind rushing past my body, through my hair, through my fully restored left eyebrow. I turned and saw him huffing and puffing it up the street.

He shouted, "How long we going to run, Wayne?"

I jogged backward and shouted, "Until I get tired. And I'm not tired yet."

I turned around and kept running, leaving him in my wake.

Full of bottomless energy.

Thunderous hope.

After another half mile, he turned back.

"Okay, I'm turning back," he shouted. "I'm not deserting you, but my knee is killing me."

I gave him a thumbs-up and kept going. Moving forward. I couldn't help that a smile took over my face. I checked the wide blue sky for planes and, sure enough, there were two. Crisscrossing a section of sky, leaving behind white foam trails.

And I got a burst of energy and felt like my muscles were full of jet fuel.

So I launched into a sprint.

Sprinting.

Running.

Smiling.

Run.

Run.

Run.

Run.

Running without fear.

Running out in the open.

Running because I wanted to.

Do you know what that kind of run felt like?

I'll tell you.

It felt an awful lot like flying.

ACKNOWLEDGMENTS

Writing this book was a lot of fun. It was made more enjoyable by many wonderful people.

I'm continuously grateful to my terrific agent, Julia Kenny, whose early enthusiasm for Wayne's story buoyed me. Thank you so much to my editor, Bethany Strout, for your wise guidance, sharp editorial eye, and kind encouragement. I feel blessed to work with you. Heaps of gratitude and thanks to Lisa Yoskowitz, Victoria Stapleton, Jenny Choy, Barbara Bakowski, Ashley Mason, and Maggie Edkins. The entire team at Little, Brown Books for Young Readers is top-notch. True story.

Thanks to Bernie Alves, Warren Ayers, Abby (the best dog ever) Chapman, CJ and Momo Chapman, Matt Chapman, Oliva Chapman, Dave Diotalevi, Gloria Harris,

Polly Holoyke, Tim (weedwacker) Mason, Julie Neinast, Mary Paj, Patrick "Mr. Q" Quinlan, Les Rosenblatt, Susan Thornton, Sean Vance, and especially Sandra and Eldon Youngblood. Each of you inspired me in important and unique ways that are woven deeply into this book. Special thanks to American Airlines First Officer and Air Force Lt. Colonel Gavin Tade for your insights and encouragement and, most important, your passion for flight and service to our country.

To all of my family, I love you and thank you for supporting me. For my Heavenly Father, for everything. And finally, a special thanks to my readers. Where once I had a file full of rejection letters, I now have a file full of letters from readers. Do you know how cool that is? Pretty cool.